RO WIJEWICKRAMA

THE AWAKENED MIND – PROPHECY

BOOK 1

To the LITTLE GIRL on top of the Mango Tree at 174

Contents

Dreams Resurrected

The year 1985

The gorgeous sun's rays pierced through the early morning fog that blanketed the riverbank, beckoning the local wildlife to come out and play. The mist shimmered and danced across the crystal clear stream, with silver fish gracefully darting through its depths. A beautiful flock of many-colored birds pieced an intricate quilt against the deep blue sky as they soar and dipped above the water in unison. As if joining a chorus, a single owl hooted its melodious song to its companion in the treetops. The branches of the fruit trees slowly swayed and curled in harmony as they eagerly reached for the sunlight – each movement dropped more of their yellowy leaves into the stream below. Not far away, a thin trail of smoke rose from an old house, built centuries ago with clay and heavily covered by vines. All around, musky spices combined with wood smoke on the breeze filling this jungle paradise with vast amounts of wonderful aromas. This secret forgotten place had been apart from civilization for many years, inhabited only by a small tribal group named Lyon, meaning Lion. This unassuming village was settled atop a flat land which housed fourteen homes, bursting with their own unique culture and ways of life.

A group of men with white paint on their skin bustled around, helping their neighbors repair the wall by mixing mud and water into a malleable paste. Meanwhile, another pack of men emerged from the depths of the forest, their arms laden with dinner for the evening. All of them were painted in the same manner, except for the oldest among them who had a unique design adorning his chest; it marked him as the leader of his tribe.

The women had fresh flowers woven through their hair and draped about their neck while clothed in straw skirts that billowed softly in the breeze. They moved around and near the fire pits, stirring pots of bubbling vegetables and freshly cooked meat as the aroma filled the air. Another group fussed over family members, ensuring everyone was fed and taken care of.

Some kids ran around playing with toys they crafted them-selves, others picked fruits and vegetables while older children collected firewood to add to the blaze. If one stood still long enough, they could feel and smell the rich grass blowing in the wind, hear the soothing sound of water gushing from a nearby river and birds singing joyous harmonies above them. The willow trees almost seemed to dance with each gust, rustling and scattering petals all around. This was a happy place - one where peace reigned supreme. But not that day.

That day was one of pure terror, a cold and stillness settling in the air that made it difficult to breathe. The sky rumbled with thunder as dark storm clouds rolled in from far away lands, casting an ominous silhouette across the small village at the foot of the mountain. All of nature went eerily silent, no birds sang and no flowers bloomed. A feeling of dread and panic filled each person's soul, as something sinister had invaded their home. Man against man stopped for a moment to take in what was happening - people were running wildly around, trying desperately to find safe shelter for their families. Men, old and young alike, stood up to defend their homes but discovered that their weapons were powerless against a force they hadn't seen before - attackers who seemed like darker versions of themselves. Even then you could feel a fatalistic gloom cling in the air, women lay lifeless on the ground clutching onto their children until life left them just as quickly as it had come.

"Help... Help." a woman yelled.

Some ran through the dark clouds of smoke trying to put out the fire.

"Evil is coming... Run..." yelled, another villager.

Screams echoed through the small village, its once peaceful tranquility upended by the crackle of flames. The heat was suffocating, and so was the terror. A villager yelled in agony as he was burned alive, his flesh seared into oblivion. Others frantically ran through the thick smoke of his funeral pyre, searching desperately for some form of aid. But there was none to be found.

A woman cried out, her voice filled with grief and confusion, seeking her children in a panic. She had no idea if they were still alive or already taken by the merciless blaze. The death toll rose quickly; some were hung, others butchered, while many simply dropped dead from exhaustion and fear.

The fire seemed to have no origin; it sprouted suddenly, without warning or logic. It raged on relentlessly, destroying everything and everyone in its path at an alarming pace that defied understanding. No one knew how to contain it or stop it from spreading further.

The people tried to escape from something unseen but clearly present; possessed individuals who cut down any who dared get too close to them with vicious glee. Chaos reigned supreme as buildings collapsed and families were separated in the frenzy.

The inferno stretched on seemingly endlessly, leaving nothing but ash and ruin in its wake. It was a disaster of apocalyptic proportions - something no one could ever forget.

At a distance, on top of the rock, was a young girl, her tiny frame no more than five years old. Her raven hair was tied back with a pink ribbon, and she wore small blue jeans and a pink t-shirt adorned with printed butterflies near the bottom right corner. She brought her hand up to cover her mouth as dust filled the air while frantically wiping away the mud that smudged her jeans. Her eyes were full of terror and tears cascaded down her dirty face as she watched in horror the chaos below, where flames shot up from the ground engulfing all that once stood there where her friends and family used to live.

The little girl had seen enough. Instinctively, she got up and sprinted towards what seemed like an impossible entrance, hidden behind trees and overgrown grass with vines hanging down from above. Even when it was visible, it looked out of place; but this desolate passage offered some sort of refuge for the frightened child. As she entered into the darkness of the cave, a long forgotten road appeared before her yet still strangely unfamiliar to everyone but her.

In that dark path, the original settlers were unknown insects and other bugs she had not heard of before crawled beneath the overgrown grass and weeds. She was cold and afraid, her knees trembled in fear as she walked slowly down the path, touching the walls as a guide that led her to the unknown. To her surprise, another figure hovered within its walls.

She stumbled upon the vast chamber of the cave, and gasped in astonishment. The old lanterns barely illuminated the space, yet it was enough to reveal countless carvings, sculptures, images, and messages covering each wall. It felt like history itself was preserved within these walls, shrouded in time and dust.

The little girl could not help but stare in amazement at this sight before her. With an explorer's curiosity and awe, she examined every inch of this unknown world. At that moment, a sudden burst of light entered from the other side of the cavity, and what she saw made her heart skip a beat. Standing confidently ahead of her was a woman, around thirty-three years old with tan skin and long black hair. She wore blue jeans – shreds and patches making them look more like rags than clothes – and a tattered tight-fitting black shirt, along with a leather holder strapped onto her right thigh which held a large knife. Her waist cinched tightly with two guns and bullets clinking inside their cases. From her gaze to her attire, it felt as if G. I Jane had just stepped out of the pages of a comic book.

The little girl timidly tiptoed closer, cautiously observing the woman. The tall rocks, , fallen logs, and broken sculptures hampered her view; yet, as the intense breathing of the mystery figure reached her, she found herself inching forward with insatiable curiosity, wanting to see what the woman had in her hands. Suddenly, an unnatural radiance erupted and came into sight as if someone had ignited a magnesium flashbulb. Everything around them was engulfed by its blinding light. She spun around with increasing fear, witnessing a wall of white-hot energy that seared through her vision. An invisible force field pressed down on her like a heavy weight, contorting her body in all directions until she collapsed onto the floor with a thunderous thud. Her entire body quivered with tension as tingles shot up her spine and the pressure of the air changed dramatically. All she could do now was lay there, hoping against hope that this would all be over soon.

What You See Is Not What You Get

I woke up in a heartbeat, my long black hair plastered against my face. I was drenched in sweat and had just had a dream but I couldn't remember what it was about. My heart was racing so quickly that my breath caught in its throat, as if I had swallowed a fish bone. The thumping of my heart echoed like drums throughout my body until it felt like the organ itself was going to explode. Still awake, I looked at my digital clock sitting on my side table illuminated by the moonlight that shone through my window. It read 2:33 am.

Why are you awake again Kailie? I thought to myself in frustration. My sheets were a mangled mess around me as I rubbed my eyes dry and took in the cool air from outside. A silent mist was rolling through the canyon, and I could feel it moving across me as if it too was looking for some way to stay warm. It was still early in the morning, so no one else would be up until at least six—if they ever made it out of bed at that hour anyway. I slowly sat up on my bed, my body was chilled despite being covered well by flannel fabric, which gave my skin goosebumps and stiffness when I pushed myself out of bed to go look out into the night sky. As soon as my feet hit the ground, the floorboards creaked under my bare feet. My fingers ran through my sweaty hair and tangled it even more. I wiped the cold beads of sweat off of my forehead with the back of my hand as if I could wipe away the drips that were still clinging from my hairline. I made my way to the window, studying the night sky every few steps. When my eyes first landed on the glass panes, I was expecting something to be there since that's how most nights felt when I woke up in the middle of them. All I received was silence, a stillness of the night with only the moon guiding me through the foggy street lights.

I stood by the window, looking out into the blackness. The stars glittered across in the sky like tiny fireflies winking their eternal glow. I wondered if my mother was still alive, what she was doing, and what she looked like. If she wanted me to be adopted; maybe she was still looking for me? I didn't look anything like my foster parents - it was obvious that I must have been from a different race. My almond-shaped eyes were wide apart, and unlike my foster parents, I had high cheekbones that added depth to my dimpled cheeks. I couldn't help but wonder though, what my biological mom looked like. Despite coming from a different race, it wasn't an issue that mattered to me. However, it would have been comforting to know where I came from or who my birth parents were.

My foster dad had died four years earlier after suffering a heart attack whilst jogging in the park. But he and I shared a very deep bond, one that not even death could break. Memories of him were still fresh in my mind, and I couldn't imagine not having him in my life. I had nothing in common with my foster parents except for the love they showered me with; they always made me feel like I belonged. They had given me so much more than just food and shelter - they gave me a home, something I never knew existed until they took me in. Sometimes, when I looked at them closely enough, watching their every move and how they treated each other, I saw glimpses of myself reflected back at me - small mannerisms here and there that hinted at something deeper than blood or genetics. But even though they loved me unconditionally, the question of where I came from remained unanswered and led to many sleepless nights filled with worry and wonder.

I have seen this dream eight times. I don't understand why I keep seeing it, falling asleep to it as if someone were calling my name, hovering above me and telling me that all is well without my realizing that I am dreaming. The heat, the wind, and the pain were all very real sensations. "Is someone trying to call me?" I thought. I struggled with the thoughts imprisoning my mind because I knew that a voice was calling to me, someone was whispering for my attention.

I shook my head, trying to rid myself of the ridiculous thought. "Come on Kailie, You're no superhero," I told myself. My fingers held on tightly to the thin gold necklace around my neck, feeling every groove and curve as it glinted in the moonlight. The chain felt cool and smooth beneath my skin, but not cold; its texture somehow gentle and comforting. The pendant was a charm of some sort, six points surrounding a star design with an inscription running over each point in another language - perhaps Latin? I couldn't remember where I got it from or who had given it to me. It had been a present at one time, that much I remembered, but when? How long ago? All these questions unanswered.

As the thoughts ran through my mind, I realized that I could feel a warmth spreading through my veins - a feeling of strength and invincibility building inside of me. Was there something more than just a simple piece of jewelry here?

I sank back down onto my bed, the soft fabric of my sheets pooling around me. The room was dark and oppressive, and I felt as though it were swallowing me whole. My mind whirled with thoughts of what I had just seen, twisting and turning like vines in a dense jungle. I gazed up at the ceiling, staring at the shadows that seemed to shift and writhe like living things. Once again, I found myself consumed by the darkness of the night, feeling its emptiness wash over me. I knew I needed sleep, but my body refused to cooperate as my mind continued to race, chasing after elusive answers to questions I couldn't quite frame. With effort, I forced myself to close my eyes and drift off into unconsciousness.

Vision Of His Face

Back in 1985, the little girl was on the ground, lungs burning as if they were engulfed with fire. Smoke and ash particles clogged her throat, making it impossible to take in air. Each breath felt like breathing in scorching sulfuric acid, causing her to gasp for breath in agony. Her strength began to slowly leave her body as she coughed and wheezed desperately, but no amount of coughing could expel the heavy smoke that had already penetrated her system. A thick cloud of smoke bellowed through the hallway. All around her, flames licked whatever remained of the once trusted historical cave which she named her safe haven. Beads of sweat trickled down her face - a combination of fear and the heat from the raging fire. The little girl then mustered up enough energy to turn herself over onto her right side, only to be met by a sight she hoped she'd never witness—the woman who had been her mother lay lifeless on the floor. Blood rushed out from every orifice, painting a gruesome picture as each drop seeped into the uneven rock bed beneath her. Despite all this tragedy surrounding her, she dragged herself closer to her mother's body and touched her cold hand one last time in farewell before trying to escape.

Her eyes fluttered open and closed. Her world was spinning, and she felt horrible. It was as if she were drunk, except that she hadn't eaten anything or had anything to drink for hours. Suddenly, a man grabbed her by her arms and dragged her to the far wall of the cavern, her little feet leaving a trail on the stone floor behind her. She struggled to free herself, but it was no use.

She felt herself fading in and out of existence. Her eye caught a glimpse of the orange color brighten by sunlight coming through the trees, like an angelic ray of hope sent from above. She forced her eyes to open wider and wider but all she saw was a bloody, raw hand before everything went dark again. Visions of his face swam in her mind, and for a moment it brought her some solace to know that if only for one second she could see him before leaving this reality forever, maybe the pain wouldn't be as unbearable. To know who was trying to save her was all she wanted to know, but soon enough reality overtook her and all was gone.

The Gypsy

The shrill sound of my alarm clock sliced through the silence, its piercing seven-note sequence increasing in frequency with each unfeeling chime. I hurled myself out of bed from its first tick, but by the fourth chime I had already lost my chance for a snooze. I cursed at my own lethargy as recognition of another morning squandered to late rising sunk in; this was the second and third time since last week that my attempts for a timely wake-up were thwarted.

"Shit," I yelled looking at the clock, "I'm late again."

The cold sensation of my toothbrush against my tongue was quickly forgotten as I stumbled forward, attempting to rush out the door to work that I had apparently already forgotten about. My right toe collided with the wooden leg of the end table next to my bedroom door and a sharp pain surged through the side of my foot, blinding me as it shot up my leg. The intensity of it was almost unbearable, like a fusillade of bullets pounding against brain tissues in a frozen battlefield. Cold beads of sweat broke out against my forehead as I ignored the pain for now; time seemed to have sped up all around me and there wasn't a moment to spare. All I could do was grab my coat desperately from the closet hook before sprinting down the hallway. But even this effort was thwarted by my overslept morning – I had completely forgotten to brush my hair, meaning I couldn't pull it into a neat braid or low ponytail to shield myself from the outside elements. The morning air swept against my cheeks like stinging needles, ushering its frigid misty breath over any exposed flesh.

This was not like me at all. Lack of sleep, mixed with an overabundance of nervous energy had taken me away from myself, which made me shout curses at everyone in my path,

"Get out, move, out of my way," I yelled while running down the street.

I darted around a cluster of teenagers who were lounging on the corner and cut through an alleyway that smelled like spoiled milk.

I stumbled onto the bustling side of town, just in time to witness the homeless man across the street pulling up his trousers from a freshly relieved bladder. The sun bore down mercilessly on me as I frantically hailed for a taxi cab. After what felt like an eternity, a double-decker tour bus finally halted in front of me and hordes of perspiring tourists came spilling out into the street.

The acrid smell of sweat hung heavy in the air as they hurried past me to take pictures of sights that had been captured multiple times before them. My clothes were drenched with sweat as I pushed myself forward with each labored gasp. My inner voice urged me not to give up - if I didn't make my move now then things would remain stagnant forever. Finally after fifteen minutes of running against the clock, I reached my destination; the cafe where I was supposed start working ten minutes ago.

"I know, I know, I'm sorry," I yelled before he even opened his mouth to yell at me.

Steve stood with one hand on his waist and his other arm extended, pointing at the clock in front of him. His dark eyes pierced through me. Black pants and a white T-shirt gave him a clean professional look—that is, if you were looking for a bodyguard and not a cook or waiter. He worked in the "Timeless Café" on Main Street, and he was always pleasant to work with. But when I slept in again and made it late for work, he wasn't so friendly anymore. The "Timeless Cafe" was owned by Mr. and Mrs. Dockstable, who had retired and turned the business over to Steve and their daughter Jenny. Inside the cafe were two large wooden tables on either side of the bar area. Brown ceramic countertops divided the kitchen from the dining area.

Four tables filled the floor, cracked wooden stools splayed out in front of them like an audience waiting for a show. The morning light cast a warm yellow glow on the walls and the tables, which were crowded with people on stools sipping their morning coffee before rushing off to work. In the far corner, a jukebox stood near the door alongside three gumball machines made from swirls of bright yellow and red paint and covered in stickers.

The booths were all brown leather, as if someone had decided to give the cafe a 70's theme. People sat packed together at the tables as they tried to finish up their breakfast.

"Good morning," I said with a smile and put on my black apron. "How may I help you?" The old couple quickly looked up from their menus and smiled.

"I would like one of number 4 with no cheese, one number 19, and two coffees' with no sugar please," said the old man

"Okay, not a problem. It will be about 10 minutes. I'll bring your coffee right away".

Ryan strides through the back counter holding a clear glass pitcher of water, his excitement about it evident from the way he holds the handle. We are so alike in that we each carry our desires with pride, and now I understand why. We've spent too long being afraid to put ourselves out there for the world to see, but here in this café where Ryan waits on customers day after day is my chance to tell him how much I care. The excuse I keep telling myself is that it's not the right time. He has caught me a few times checking him out but I just smile and pretend it was nothing. Ryan was my first friend from college. We have the same career aspirations so all our classes are the same.

"Hey Kailie, are you alright, you look exhausted. What's up? Not much sleep again is it?" asked Ryan

I didn't know I looked like crap, what's worse is that he noticed that I looked like crap. Well, I didn't really have a whole lot of time to put my make-up on this morning. Ryan looked good today. He looks good in anything he wears. Even if you put a garbage bag over his head and covered his long legs and muscular chest, he'll still look good but here I am looking like a drained, sleep-deprived person with probably dark eye bags under my eyes.

"Ya, I'll tell you about it later, I have to serve this quick," I told him and brushed off the question.

* * *

Inside the musty locker room, I sat on the bench in front of row after row of lockers. A bare light bulb burned above my head, giving everything an eerie glow. My toes were planted against a brown 6-foot locker next to me. The rest of the locker room was dark and empty. I loved the stillness and silence, compared to the noisy atmosphere out in the cafe.

Ryan sat in front of me on the bench, his knees spread wide around mine. He took my hand in his and gave it a tight squeeze. He hasn't been this close to me before, I could feel his breath. My heartbeat is all over the place and I am finding it so hard to suppress my feelings. I looked straight into his eyes which were gazing back at me.

"Kailie, what's going on with you? You drop plates, and yawn in front of customers and in class, are you okay?", Ryan's concerned tone made me feel safe. I want to kiss him so badly. Come on Kailie, Focus. So I took a deep breath and turned towards Ryan,

"You know I was adopted right? And I don't remember my past, but something is wrong. I can feel it in every fiber of my body. I have been having these dreams, the same dream over and over again every night, sometimes a little bit more."

In the dream I am on fire. My skin melts into nothing as the flame grows higher and hotter, until there is nothing left that resembles me except my eyes. When Ryan watches me describe this to him he frowns. His hand squeezes mine reassuringly; his dark eyes lighten with understanding, then they darken with pity. The rational side of my brain knows I am just thinking about it too much when I am awake, but the inferno rekindles when I sleep.

"I don't know, dreams that repeat themselves usually mean something. Or you might be thinking about it so much when you're awake that your subconscious keeps bringing it back to the forefront of your sleep-time thoughts."

"Maybe you're right. Maybe I'm just imagining everything..."

Ryan slid his legs into place on the bench, straddling it and facing me. He leaned in closer to kiss me, but instead he put his hands on my shoulders and gripped me tight against him. It was as if my skin could sense the heat of his flesh through my sweater. I wanted him to kiss me, desperately, but he didn't. Instead, we sat there watching each other, caught between what our bodies desired and what our minds thought would be best. "Kailie honestly, it's not the right time" I thought to myself. Getting a pity kiss isn't what I wanted, so I just sat there instead, watching him carefully as we sat in silence but grateful for the hug from my best friend. The connection between us was broken as he pulled away, looking at me with concern this time.

"Hey, if you believe it that much, there is this great gypsy we can go see... You may not believe in these things, but it could help" he whispered and I nodded still buried under his warm arms.

* * *

That sunny afternoon, the streets of Chinatown glowed with red and yellow lanterns. They were strung across the buildings as if by magic. Stores blaring Chinese music and the sharp smell of raw fish blended with boiled cabbage to spill into the air like a heavy gas. The sound of pots clanking against each other and the smells of cumin and ginger fluttered in through open windows. There were small vendors selling food on the street out of their mobile carts, and some even sold it sitting on the floor. You could see people rushing off with food inside plastic bags during their lunch break from work.

Ryan and I walked through the narrow streets to a dead end. The buildings on either side of us blocked the sunlight from falling onto the sidewalk. This part of the city was quiet, almost abandoned; the only sound was that of the occasional car or people talking in distant. In this dark corner stood a small shop, its window hidden by a tall weed. Above it was an old board that said "Madam T." There used to be more to that board, but it was old and faded. The entrance to the store was strands of beads made out of polished seashells that creaked as they swayed back and forth. Madam Theresa's shop was like a secret garden, tucked away in a forgotten corner of town. Years ago, when Madam Theresa had first opened her storefront, it had been the talk of the city—as much for its mysterious offerings as for its bright and inviting decor. But as time went on the novelty had worn off, and the shop seemed to exist in its own pocket of time, timeless and unchanging.

As Ryan and I stepped inside, we were greeted by a heavy incense scent. Inside the shop was a large table next to which sat two cashier machines. A shelf ran along another wall with various herbs in bottles lined neatly on top of it. On top of one register was a silver tray full of charms: pendants, amulets, talismans, some symbolic, some just for decoration, all for sale at $4.99 each. I stopped at a symbol with three silver circle with three points; It was so pretty; I couldn't take my eyes off it. I was ready to purchase it when a lady came up in front of me, a warm smile spread across her sun-browned face.

"Welcome, welcome!" she said in a strong but gentle voice. "What can I do for you?"

I stepped forward nervously. "I would like a reading,"

Madam Theresa nodded. "Ahhh, I see. Please, come"

"That's a triquetra," she said, pointing at the silver charm on my hand. "It's a symbol of good magic."

I nodded, her heart beating faster. Madam Theresa seemed to know things, things that I had never told anyone. She felt a strange kinship with the old woman, and her curiosity only grew as Madam Theresa continued her inspection.

Madam Theresa was an old woman who had been beautiful once. Now her face was covered in layers of makeup, which bordered on garish but was softened by the careful application. Her eyelids were blue, and her lips a matte red, her cheeks dusted with pale blush. She wore heavy earrings made of bronze-plated alloy, huge hoops that swung from one earlobe to the next like a pair of pendulums. They knocked against each other as she talked. Her hair was real but dyed a fake shade of brown, and draped across her forehead, heavily streaked with gray, was a bright red scarf. The scarf hid her thinning hairline at the back of her head. Around her neck hung another bangle of bronze-plated alloy roped through with thick twisted wire.

She also had a row of flowers on her hair on top, where two beaded chains were falling over her forehead. In the center of the forehead was a big wooden bead that threatened to fall forward into her left eye at any second. The white and red fabric of the dress swished back and forth as she walked toward the dark room, making a soothing noise with the clangs of countless tiny metal charms hanging from her arms.

"Come this way, my child" she said as she began walking towards another room connected to the shop.

Ryan and I followed her into the parlor, where an old-fashioned sofa sat facing a stage. An ornate table with glittering crystals and polished stones sat in front of it. The wood on the walls was hand carved and painted to look like gilded leaves. A fireplace stood at one end and had been lit with sweet smelling incense that lingered in the air. On a mirror above the mantle were dozens of pictures taped together, some looking twenty or so years old, others much older. We took seats on the velvet pillows that lined the couch and waited for Madam Theresa to take hers. I wasn't sure if I was ready to hear what she had to say or believe anything she said, but I was desperate and I had more questions than answers, so I reached my hand giving her permission to examine it the way she may see fit. She stared at me until I looked away from those all knowing eyes. When she spoke, her voice sounded like water flowing over pebbles.

"You don't have to do this if you're not ready, child."

Ryan moved closer and squeezed my hand. "Yes," I replied hesitantly as I steeled myself for whatever was about to happen next.

Madam Theresa looked into the creases of my palm, her eyebrows furrowed and eyes wide. She squeezed it so hard that her fingers sank into my flesh like a knife cutting through butter. I didn't know my brown skin could turn red until that time but she was digging in so hard as if to find some hidden item beneath my skin. I felt heat radiating from my hand and then seeping up my arm, a sensation that made me uncomfortable yet excited at the same time. Theresa's wrinkled face displayed deep concentration as she peered down at my palm.

I could see fear and confusion in her eyes, and when she looked back up at me she saw fear in mine, too. My heart pounded rapidly in my chest as the seconds ticked by, and Ryan held his breath next to me. The old lady suddenly got up from her chair, screaming, and took a few steps back.

Madam T's eyes widened as she shook her head and pushed me towards the door. "This can't be right... Your reading is over. You have to leave. You have to leave now," she said, her voice quivering with fear.

I pleaded with her, desperate for answers. "Please. Tell me what you see. I need to know what's going on..." But Madam T would not be swayed.

Madam T's eyes widened in fear and she pointed a quivering finger at Ryan, warning him to stay away from me. "You!! The trouble this girl is... You... Stay away from her." Her words were ominous, weighted with meaning that I couldn't begin to fathom.

I begged Madam T for guidance, my voice thick with emotion. "Please, Madam... Please... you're my only hope..."

With another step backwards, Madam T paused before issuing a grave warning of great danger that awaited me if I wasn't careful. "Great danger. Behold your life. Death might be a visitor before you find the light. It will swallow you unless you are careful... Now go. Please don't come back in here again."

Her words hung heavily in the air, sending shivers down my spine. The room seemed to spin around me as my heart rate spiked and breath came in short gasps. I stumbled out of the shop, leaving Ryan behind, and ran as fast as my legs could carry me.

* * *

I walked into my apartment and flipped on the light switch. The soft glow of early evening illuminated my living room, which was ordinarily a comforting sight. I reached for the remote to turn the TV on, but when I flipped it on, Sarah Bareilles's hauntingly sad voice wailed in anguish about how she loved a man who didn't love her back. Every time that song played, I could feel her pain as if it were my own. I quickly hit the off button, tossing the remote aside and looked at my phone which indicated 14 missed calls from Ryan. I wasn't ready to talk to him yet so I put down the phone face-down on the nightstand

and started to pace around the room biting my fingernails. My inner turmoil churned like water in a boiling pot. I walked towards the window to let in some fresh air hoping at least that would make me feel better but the loud noises of the people outside yelling were too much for me to handle. There is only one thing that would make me feel better when I feel like this. There is only one person who can calm me down. So I grabbed my phone and dialed the number without even realizing why I was gnawing on my knuckles or why I was pacing around the room.

"Hello... Pick up the phone, please... are you there." I started to talk to myself.

"Hello...." Said the voice through the phone

"Mom!!!" I said

"What's wrong honey? Are you okay?" replied Mom

I couldn't bring the words to come out of my mouth; all I could do at that moment was just cry. Even if I tried to talk I don't think mom could understand what I was saying. I was crying so much I started to stammer and I had to force myself to calm down so she could understand what I was trying to say.

"Mom." The word stuck in my throat. "I went to this gypsy lady. She told me some stuff. It's scary and this dream I've been having every day...and mom what's happening to me?"

"Darling," my mother responded, soothingly. "Don't get scared! Everything happens for a reason and there is some stuff you don't know about yourself! Some stuff we haven't talked about for years—but now it is time!"

That night, just like any other night I hugged my second pillow so tight and held on to the baseball bat before falling asleep again but then faded into another dream.

* * *

Unclear images started to appear. The older woman is now holding a crystal in her hands, the light shines through its facets and reflects against the rock walls of that dark cave. She is speaking in an ancient language while chalk-white powder is swirling in small circles around her feet. There are cracks spreading out from where she stands, leading from each tiny noise she makes, traveling across the ground and up towards the ceiling of the cave. The crystals in the walls are shaking, and one falls down from the top of the wall creating a dust cloud that fills the air within the cave.

The small girl came out of hiding and clung to her mother's leg, pulling her to stop and asking her to turn around. The girl was scared, her little heart was beating faster, and though she tried not to cry any louder than a whisper, tear after tear trickled down her cheek.

The woman was wearing a necklace around her neck with a symbol on it. Loud voices poured inside the cave, yet her calm voice mellowed and naturalized everything else; she muttered words under her breath like a lullabye or a calming mantra: 'Earth to Water, Wind to Fire'

Before she could finish reading the inscription, creatures began pouring out of the woods and attacking her. The woman looked at her daughter and was afraid for her life as blood gushed from her waist where she had been wounded; she held onto her little girl with one hand as they ran deeper into the cave.

The passage they were running into was fenced by thick weeds that grew along its length, it laid hidden away from all eyes looking for shelter, It was an old volcano crater covered by grasses long ago. Then just before their way ended abruptly they entered through a thin hole which barely allowed the little girls body to enter but it protected her.

Her mother, her face framed by a white bonnet, was saying something, almost like a whisper with all the surrounding noise. The little girl tried to listen very carefully, but the voice was too faint. She strained forward and then the dream took an unexpected turn and I woke up trying to catch my breath.

The Intruder

The clock struck 1 am, and Mrs. Logan was sitting beside her bed dressed in a pink and white nightgown, looking down at a box that she had placed earlier on her lap. Her wrinkled fingers, going through the details of the hand carvings on the box, took her back to a far distant memory. She is 5 feet 3 inches tall, fair with brown hair. The long hours spent reading books on history and mystical characters showed in her eyes reaching far back before Kailie's birth. Her youthful face was now lined by time, but it didn't detract from the smile that lay beneath it. Furthermore, she is loving, devoted, and a great friend; she is perfect.

The midnight air was like cool silk that night. The room smelled exactly like it, sweet and fresh. The light from the streetlamp outside crept through the window, making it the only light available in that room. The light was so faint that even she could barely see the content of the box. She runs her fingers through the items and looks up. She glances at the clock, debating in her mind if she should call her darling daughter but finally decide not to as she sighs a deep, unsatisfying breath, almost one of regret.

"Oh, Kailie. I didn't think I needed to open this box. But, it's only fair that you know who you really are" said Mrs. Logan to herself as she let out a long breath.

She placed the box back in a safe spot inside the closet floor, softly closed the door, and walked towards her bed. She patiently sat on her bed looking out the window, waiting for the sun to come out. She let out another sigh and laid back on her bed, ready to fall asleep.

Criiiiiikkkllleee...the floorboards creaked menacingly... She bolted upright, her heart racing in her chest. The noise stopped, but she knew someone was there. In the room's oppressive darkness, everything seemed to merge into one.

Criiiiiikkkllleee... came the noise again, this time a little louder and closer than before. Fear overtook her body as she whispered a timid,

"Who's there... ?" She peered through the thick of night towards her bedroom door, the seconds passed like hours while dread slowly crawled up her spine.

Criiiiiikkkllleee ... the floorboards creaked again...... This time she knew it for sure. It's the creak you get when your body weight moves from one leg to the other on a loose floorboard, and she knew exactly where it was coming from because she had stepped on that very same floor board over a hundred times.

"Footsteps," she whispered to herself.

Instinctively, she jumped out of bed trying to reach the door handle, desperate to lock it before whatever lurked outside could get in. But before she could even turn the handle, something unseen knocked her away with a force powerful enough to throw her across the room.

Pain surged through her fragile body as she lay on her side breathing heavily, eyes wide with terror as she registered each bruise and ache that covered her body. Her nightdress had been lifted by the impact, exposing skin between buttons that had come undone. As she rose to face the unknown she found herself shivering with fear and trembling in anticipation of what may come.

"Come here you!" roared the man with a voice that shook the foundations of the house. His appearance, though shrouded in darkness, revealed itself to be a treacherous mask: his face was covered by a thick layer of paint but underneath it all, Mrs. Logan could clearly make out light brown skin - his ears and other areas not completely smothered by the black hue. He advanced towards her like a ravenous beast, grabbing her hands and holding them so tightly behind her back that she thought they might snap off. The pain was so overwhelming, her arms felt like they were being pulled from their sockets as she screamed for mercy.

"Please don't hurt me," she begged, "I don't have any money...you can take anything from the house".

But an echoing response cut through Mrs. Logan's pleas: "We don't want your stuff", as she looked up into the nightmarish darkness, a figure began to form and step out of the shadows.

"Who are you and what do you want?" She said shakily, afraid of the dread that came with the unknown.

The Origin

About 5000 Years Ago

Time had lost its meaning in the ancient palace. The walls were on fire outside King Tomka's chambers. People ran through the palace, leaping over broken furniture and tattered tapestries to find some part of the castle that hadn't been burned by flames. Some people hunched together around a table as they decided what to do next. Others gathered at the edge of a balcony and looked into the courtyard below where men struggled, pulled at each other and cut off heads with axes and blades. Outside the palace gates, horses reared up on their hind legs and kicked out with their hooves. Their eyes rolled wildly in their sockets, and foam dripped from their muzzles. King Tomka took arms to fight the last battle he would ever fight against his own brother. He ran down a corridor with his only daughter Princess Sophie who wore full armor like a man; she walked behind him and placed her hand on his shoulder.

"My darling daughter, I need you to be safe. You know why" said the King

"I will never leave your side," said the Princess, tightening the grip on her sword and staring towards the palace doors.

"You're stubborn as your mother was," replied the King with a smile

The main hall gates opened with a bang. The sunlight shone through and glinted off the smooth crystal lining the doorway behind the tall figure who stood before them. Steam hissed from his mouth as he spoke.

"Greed has consumed you, brother. Stop this while you can," yelled the King.

"Where is the Crystal? Give it to me now..." screamed Prince Telkish. His scream roared throughout the palace echoing through the walls.

"You will have to go past me first." Yelled the King with his might.

Princess Sophie gripped her sword tighter and watched in horror as Prince Telkish stepped closer. His red eyes pierced as he looked past his brother to her. His gaze traveled down her body until she noticed that he was looking directly at her heart, and then his eyes shifted into a different color altogether: gray flecked with black like clouds over a stormy sea as waves crashed against rock cliffs under darkened skies, revealing flashes of lightning deep within their depths.

"Then that shall be" yelled the prince as he charged towards the king with his sword raised high.

The clashing of steel against steel echoed through the palace, ringing in Sophie's ears as she watched her father's brave guards fall one by one. The king staggered forward, desperately parrying each blow from the prince's blade. His feet slipping in a pool of blood that had grown quickly around him. For a moment, he looked towards his daughter and smiled before taking a fatal thrust to the heart from the prince's sword. Tears streamed down Sophie's face as her father slumped to the ground.

Tears seeped through the seams of her eyelids.

"Father...?" she whined. Her words were barely audible, drowned out by the thunderous crackle of lightning in front of her.

A brilliant light, piercing and pure, struck her eyes like a spear of light. The light was so bright it seemed to have no edges or details across its surface; it was like seeing from inside a star. Covering your eyes would not help you. The light filled the room and burned away all colors except white and then,

Princess Sophie along with the crystal disappeared and was never to be seen or heard again.

Jonathan James

Inside Mrs. Logan's house in the early hours of the intrusive morning, the dark silhouette made its way toward her, making himself visible. A tall man stepped into the light wearing a black shirt and a dark brown overcoat. He was a man who looked like he had lived a hard life—a black scar stretched across his left eye and his right cheek torn and purple as if it would never heal.

"I am Jonathan James" sounded the man looking down at Mrs. Logan with his hands in his pocket, he stared down at her as she struggled to raise herself up in her chair so that she could look into his eyes.

"What do you want" Said Mrs. Logan, now ready for anything that might happen next because she wasn't going to give in without a fight.

"Your Daughter... I want your daughter. Her past, for my future. I know you hold her secret. Where is she... I know she is the heiress... tell me now, or you're dead." Yelled Jonathan

Mrs. Logan's thoughts scattered in a thousand directions. She could remember only one thing– the box she had looked at earlier and was determined not to even glance in that direction as she feared for her daughter's safety.

"I am Jonathan James," he said, his voice steady and even.

"What do you want?" she asked suspiciously.

He was smiling now; it made her skin crawl. She didn't feel like she could sit up straight anymore; she thought her spine would break if she moved just an inch.

"Your daughter... I want your daughter. I want your daughter- her past, for my future. I know that you hold her secret; where is she? Tell me now or I will kill you here and now," he screamed at her.

"I don't know anything more," she pleaded with shaking voice, her eyes darting about the room like a pinball, trying to land on something that would stop this man from hurting her.

"We wanted children so badly that Social Services took her and gave her to us; we didn't ask questions because we were so grateful for having a daughter at last. Please don't hurt me, please let me go! I really don't know anything else. You have got to believe me!"

"Liar!" He shouted louder than before, making the loose picture frame on the wall fall to the ground and shatter. "She is your daughter."

"No, really," pleaded Mrs. Logan with tears streaming down her face, "I don't know anything more."

Holding her face, "Let you go... how can I let you go when you have seen who I am," Jonathan said. He was sizing up the woman in front of him. She looked like she had no fight left in her. Her face was pasty white and her eyes were wide open, no longer filled with hope.

"I can't have you running around ruining my plans now, can I?" he asked Mrs. Logan. His voice resonated from his chest and into the silence of the room.

Mrs. Logan's eyes still widely opened, she gently closed her eyes and started to pray for a way out of this nightmare. Soft-spoken sermons were not enough to save her life. But, to save Kailie she prayed.

"Well, then there is no use for you anymore, is there."

Pulling out his gun, James shot her without pausing or reflecting on her last words; he knew what he had come here for—and that didn't include changing his mind or finding any reason that would justify not getting it.

Jonathan ordered his men to tidy everything up and then they walked out the door.

Mrs. Logan didn't stop praying. Unable to protect her daughter, she prayed and hoped that Kailie would find the hidden box inside her closet.

Her legs turned to rubber and then her hands; her heartbeat slowed to a distant gallop, pounding slower and slower. Still praying, Mrs. Logan took her last breath, leaving all behind but taking the most important piece of information with her forever.

The Phone Call

Waking up at five thirty in the morning is not my idea of a great start to the day. I lay in bed staring at the digital red numbers on my alarm clock, which read 5:30 am. I half-opened one eye and glanced at the bright screen, a sense of resentment welling up inside me. Before I could bury myself deeper under my comforter, the high-pitched trill of my phone cut through the air. I threw back the covers and with an anxious frown reached for my black cordless phone next to my baseball bat. What idiot was calling me at this time of the morning? I thought. With bleary eyes barely open, I stumbled through everything on my night table as I snatched up my glass of water and my alarm clock, turning them over in my haste before finally reaching for the phone. The cool plastic felt good against my fingers. It was surely unexpected to wake up and receive a call so early in the morning on a Sunday, especially since no one really calls this number before 9 am on any day, and no one ever phones me on this landline.

"Hello...." The deep voice that emerged from my throat was followed by a little cough, the scrapes of my throat like someone dragging their nails over rocks in a sandpaper blackboard screech. I managed to say softly with an unhampered, well-rested deep voice.

"Hello." It was still dark outside; the white curtains in my room were blowing like a small boat at sea, floating on the gentle breeze coming through the open window. Aunt Lara's faint voice came through the phone.

"Kailie. This is your aunt Lara..."

Aunt Lara is mom's younger sister. Younger by two minutes. If you had seen them together, you wouldn't believe they were twins, not till you looked in their eyes and saw the twinkle of a shared secret. You might have missed the family connection if it weren't for the quirk of their lips, as though they shared a joke no one else could hear. Mom was a small woman with brunette hair that fell in soft waves around her heart-shaped face. She wore dresses with bright flowers in the prints, and she smelled like freshly baked bread. Aunt Lara was tall, thin, brown in skin color, and with black hair that fell gracefully down her back to just above her waist. Her cheekbones were sharp, like knife blades, but she smiled easily and often. When I was little she would carry me on her back through the forest, high above the undergrowth and deeper into the trees than any sane mother would allow. She loved to sing too. Sometimes I would hear her singing to herself softly or sometimes loudly out on our porch or when we went for rides in the car.

"Aunt Lara, it's early. Is everything alright?" I asked in a daze

"I'm afraid not, dear. It's your mother. She has passed. I'm so sorry." Aunt Lara sobbed through the phone.

My heart shattered into a million pieces and my blood chilled solid as ice. It suddenly became difficult to breathe. The world seemed to tilt sideways and I clung to the comforter as if somehow it could hold me up on its soft folds and prevent me from tumbling down into the darkness below.

"What..." I am now fully awake and quickly sat on the bed to ensure I heard her right

In the panic of my mind, all sorts of questions flooded.

"How? When? Why? Are you Sure?" All I could think of is what would happen to me now that she was gone

"Yes darling. I came over to meet her for our morning walk. But, the front door was open. Your mother was shot in her room. The police are here and investigating the whole place."

Aunt Lara and mom enjoyed their morning walks. It came as a daily ritual for them. They would walk for 3 miles just talking and finish it off at the local coffee shop for breakfast.

Tears flowed down my cheeks and into my mouth, salty like sea water but tasting more bitter than the most rotten apple core. Choking on those tears of mine, I clutched at the phone some more and sat there hugging it tight to my chest.

My heart pounded out of control, and all I could do was gasp for breath between sobs.

"Oh Mom..."

* * *

Everything around me was dark. Only the box about to be lowered into the ground was swathed in light. I couldn't remember crossing through the threshold of the church, and I didn't realize how many people had arrived to pay their final respects to my mother. The priest's voice drowned out all other sounds around me. I didn't know how long I was standing there staring at my mom's coffin. There were so many things I wanted to talk to her about.

I kept trying not to cry as his words shot toward me like pelting rain, but when he began preaching, the tears seeped from my eyes down my face. I tried so hard to hold them in, but they slipped out anyway and ran slowly over my cheeks. I quickly wiped it off my face before anyone could see, but Ryan noticed the change in my heartbeat as I looked back at the coffin. He grabbed my hand and squeezed it to comfort me. I am so glad Ryan was here for me. I honestly wouldn't know how to get through this without him. I took the single white rose I had in my hand and laid it on top of the coffin. The workers leveraged the rough wooden box six feet below the surface, down into the cool dark earth where she would rest with her ancestors until she returned.

Ryan and I stood off to the side as the diggers worked, with their headlamps beaming down into the hole. The workers had lowered ropes and pulled up metal braces to keep the rough coffin steady inside while it was being buried.

Heavy clouds skated above the sky and rained softly on the earth. This sheltering layer of gray rain allowed us all to pay our last respects without having to worry about getting wet. The day was warm, so no one minded a little rain under their hats. In a faraway distant by a tree was a dark figure, the features of this man were unclear as he was wearing a large overcoat and a hat. I noticed that Ryan was staring into the distant corner where someone stood. He slowly lifted his hand–a warning–and held it out for me to see his palm facing up.

"What is it?"

Ryan glanced at me and shook his head and stared back out towards the tree. I am not sure what he was looking at but when I looked in the same direction there was no one there.

"What is it?" I asked again.

"Nothing. I thought I saw something. Never mind... Let's go"
Replied Ryan

He turned his head one more time and we walked away still holding my hand as I turned around one more time to look at my mom who I was leaving behind.

$$* * *$$

By the time I walked back to my mom's house from the cemetery, my face had been twisted into a nest of feelings. People had already flooded in. Aunt Lara was greeting everyone and thanking them for coming. Ryan was helping out by clearing the used plastic cups kept on every counter by the guests. I stood by the staircase dressed in my black dress leaning against the wall, pretending it to be my pillar of strength. I felt a hand on my shoulder and turned around to see an old gentleman looking down at me. His cheeks were ruddy and his eyes three times larger than normal dwarfed his face. He gave me a gentle pat on the arm as if to offer his condolences and said,

"Deepest sympathies."

I barely lifted my head acknowledging his presence. My voice was soft as I replied, "Thank you very much."

He held my hand tightly and said "She was a good woman...a shame how she died." The gentleman replied.

I nodded while raising my head, looking past him over to the old wooden shelves that housed her favorite books. But, the pain was too much to bear, so I left the so-called black coven downstairs and walked upstairs to my mother's room.

As I slid the old iron key into the lock, I didn't know how long I had been standing outside her room door. My heart fluttered like a bird in my chest and refused to rest, and my legs burned with exhaustion. With a daydream of hope of still finding her alive and the determination of finding her killer, I walked inside the room. The heavy, musty air wrapped around me like a blanket, but it was not enough to distract from the smell that hit me as soon as I opened the door: death.

"I will avenge her death" I softly whispering to myself.

The police had removed mom's body and the "crime scene" tapes, but there was still an emptiness in the air. Aunt Lara got the house scrubbed, removing the blood stains from the carpet. But, everything else in the room was untouched. The chair turned in exactly the same angle, like mom could walk back through the door at any moment. Her comb was still on her dressing table, her towel still on her clothes rack, her shoes right where she left them, and even the air still smelled of her favorite perfume. It seemed like she was still there, dwelling among all that moved.

I slowly sat on mom's bed, took a deep breath, and looked around trying to absorb this new reality.

"What do I do with all her stuff"

A faint voice, come through the door as Aunt Lara, walked into the room

"Are you okay?"

"Yes Aunty... I just needed to talk to her about some stuff. Some things... just unanswered." I replied in frustration and disappointment.

Aunt Lara stood near the doorway. Her black skirt hung just below her knees and was paired with a long sleeve blouse that covered every curve of her body. A silver headband held back her shoulder-length hair.

"Is it about your dream?"

I was stunned for a moment. How did Aunt Lara know about

my dreams? What did Mom tell her? Better yet, what did Mom know that I didn't? I quickly looked at her with my mouth open.

"You... You know about my dreams?"

Aunt Lara sat beside me on the bed, holding my hand. I could feel her concern for me like a warm wind flowing from her body to mine.

I nodded and tried to pull my hand away, but she held me tighter. For some reason, it felt like there was a 'but' coming in this conversation.

"Yes I do, but she also told me that there is some stuff you needed to find out on your own... she didn't tell me what it was." Aunt Lara gently placed her warm, comforting hand on mine and kissed my forehead before leaving the room, while stating,

"Come downstairs when you're ready. People are starting to leave now." I nodded with agreement and started gazing around the room.

"Find out... What do I need to find out? What did she mean. And what is this big secret that my mom couldn't even tell her own twin sister. Come on Kailie... this is not the time to think about this stuff" I thought to myself, the heat of frustration rising up in my chest.

Moving from one side of the room to the next and running my hands over every piece of furniture, I found nothing. Suddenly my fingers grazed against something cold and smooth under a pile of jewelry on my mother's dressing table. In a hurry I pushed aside all the things that were scattered there and found a shiny bronze key that reminded me of something that you would see in a victorian novel from the nineteenth century. With an eyebrow raised in curiosity and a skeptic feeling building inside, I took the old bronze key that was relatively taller than the other keys.

"A Key... ..... A Key to what... I'll ask Aunt Lara later on..." I told myself before placing the key inside my pocket, but it would not be secure for long. In her closet her shoes were organized and color coded on the rack next to the dressing table. I love her shoes it ranged from major designers in all shades and colors. Next to it were the sliding doors that opened into her large closet. Mom had great taste in clothes; she always dressed well and was presentable on any occasion. Clearly it didn't run in the family as I am always running around just picking whatever is clean as opposed to being planned the day before like mom was. Her favorite dresses hung from the hangers, each one made of a different material; some were sequined like ball gowns while others were matte or shiny or smooth or woven or plain. They draped over the rods in graceful lines, waiting for her return. I ran my hands through her clothes, it still had mom's smell. I couldn't take it anymore and I accidentally found myself crying while hugging mom's clothes. It may be that I held it in during the funeral that it's coming out like the flood gates had just opened. Even though I told myself not to be emotional, I failed because emotional is exactly what I was at that moment. The dresses fell in a heap beside me as they slid off their hangers and onto me where I sat weaving between them on the floor. Finally able to breathe again, I sucked down air and stood up, straightening up the mess with shaking hands until they were once again on their proper hangers. The scent infused itself into my hands when my fingers brushed against the soft fabrics.

On the right hand corner of the floor there were three boxes. Ever since Aunt Lara told me that I needed to find myself, I had become more and more inquisitive of everything around me. It looked like I was conducting an autopsy on my own life, specifically my past. The red metal box with black circles, right at the bottom, was the first I examined. Inside the oval-shaped container were mom's old ribbons, parts of fabric, buttons and needles. My mom loved crafting, It was a skill she learned from her grandmother. She tried to teach me once but I never sat in one place long enough to learn. I regret it now though, wish I had let her teach me at least that way I would have more memories with her.

I moved on to the second box - A dark brown wooden box with a gleaming pearl-white Indian design running around the four edges of the box. I tried to lift the lid by force, but it stayed shut. Frustrated, I moved onto the third box, which was black. Inside were mom's favorite pair of 400-dollar shoes. The pink and orange heels glowed under the clear plastic top of the shoebox. I lifted out one of her silk shoes and felt its softness between my fingers. I knew at that moment that I would never be able to wear her heels. Returning to the second box, I examined it even more closely than before. There was no lock anywhere to be seen; just the small groove in the middle of one of the designs along the sides of the box. The groove held a thin metal pin, like a bar through a window sill. Pressing down on the pin made another part of the box come up slightly..

Hmmmmm.... What is this... a puzzle box.... A keyhole... What is mom hiding... Why didn't mom tell me or at least Aunt Lara, I thought to myself

I suddenly remembered the old key I hid in my pocket earlier. I looked at the bronze metal object in the palm of my hand and thought to myself, that can't be it, why would mom need to hide anything? My heart was pounding inside my chest. I couldn't wait any longer. I needed to know what was inside, although I wasn't sure if it was safe. So, with one rapid gesture, I placed the mystery key inside the hole below the lid of the strange wooden box and turned it clockwise. The designs on the four corners of the box propped out and allowed me to open the strangely heavy lid.

"Story books.... drawings... toys... what is all this...why was it all locked up. What's mom's journal doing inside this box?"

The book had hardly any entries. The first few pages were blank, as I flipped through them, the paper felt stiff and almost white in my calloused hands. There was just one entry in the middle of the book.

15th July 1986

Social services handed Kailie to us. She was 6 years old, and all she said was 'It's not over', 'bright light' and she never spoke of her parents. We promised that we would raise her as our own. The following day Kailie started preschool. Her teacher told us that things might be a bit rough for the first month because she didn't talk to anyone nor did she play with the other kids. I hoped for the time being that Kailie felt safe with us till she was ready to face the truth about herself. No one really knew much about her past except for me, and I would take that knowledge to my grave if it came down to it. If anything happened to her or if an explanation became necessary, then so be it.

I was stunned by this journal entry, but far more confused than before. "What's 'not over'? What is this bright light I spoke of? Why don't I have any memory of my parents? Could they be alive?

What's it that I need to be ready for? So many questions, and no one to answer them. Why have I been left in the dark all these days, like a outsider? Was the gypsy lady correct when she said there was something so terrible about me that I would not want to know?

Heavenly Advice

That night, I placed the treasure box under my bed. The box was usually shuffled with other boxes full of memorabilia that were stacked underneath but tonight it seemed like a good place to hide things and I went to sleep that night hugging my trusty baseball bat.

* * *

Back in the Cave – 1985

The older woman bends over the little girl, her face lined with worry and frustration. Her eyes are soft but strained, as if she has suffered a tremendous loss. She drops to one knee and beckons the child closer.

"You are key to your generation," she says softly. "Don't forget Awana. Promise me. Now go. I will always be there for you when you least expect it."

"I promise, but I am scared..." replied the little girl whipping her tears that fell down her dirty face leaving marks along the way.

"I know my love, I will always be there. Now go." said the

woman bravely, indicating they didn't have time left for what was coming.

The little girl runs away from her mother but still within her sight, she hides behind a rock. What she sees next is an experience beyond her, outside of all reason or sympathy. A creature with a long beak-like mouth, sharp teeth who was dressed in a black overcoat grabbed the woman by her arm and placed a knife on her neck. He screamed at her; spit flecked her face as his voice bellowed out of his fit chest.

"Where's the Key?... tell me,"

"You will never find it." replied the woman with strength and continued to look in the direction of the little girl.

A surge of determination flew through her body, and she reached for her necklace. She swung it across the creature's face, scaring him across the left eye... The silver pendant was suspended on a rawhide cord strung through two petrified gryphon talons, and it swung away and fell into the dark rock that was carved into a cave.

"Then you will die" screamed the creature.

He turned his attention from the woman to the sky above as he broke the woman's neck. Her lifeless body fell to the floor, at that very moment, there was a change in the air. Every ray of light was sucked up by a vortex of darkness; the eerie cold in the cave became bitter and numbed every nerve ending.

The creature placed its foot on top of her body indicating to the world its victory. Silence seemed to cover everything like a thick fog while he roared loudly.

"Roarrrrrrrrrrrrrrrrrr........."

All who were present to witness the evil doing of this creature were left downhill to continue with their journey, as their purpose of staying there was no longer required after the woman was killed. The little girl slowly crept out of the cave on her hands and knees, picking up the necklace that was on the floor. She got to her feet and started walking towards the woman who was lying lifeless on the floor. Tears rolled down her face, as she calls out while shaking the woman as if to wake her from a deep sleep. "Mama, ... Mama. Wake up. We have to go... Please, Mama, Wake up."

The ground began to shake under her feet as she looked at the lifeless body in front of her Her eyes caught a glimmer in an open crevice below them and then heard a loud boom! Boom! Boom! A light so bright that it blinded the little girl who fell to the floor out of balance.

* * *

I woke up terrified and full of tears, my mouth open wide to catch the breath that choked me. Oh my god, that necklace, it's the same one I have, as a matter of fact, it's the exact one. Is that how I got it? Am I that little girl or is it someone in my past? Who is that woman? If it's me, why don't I remember anything? If not, how can anyone explain all these dreams I have been having and the necklace around my neck? Why isn't there anyone to answer my questions? My heart was pounding; every breath shook into ragged gasps for air. I sat there still for what seemed like hours before I finally cooled down enough to breathe normally again.I quickly bent over and checked under the bed to see if her treasure box was still there.

"Until I find out what's going on. This will go everywhere I go." I told myself as I placed it inside her backpack.

It took forever to fall asleep with so many questions buzzing through my thoughts but they weren't important if I couldn't sleep so I forced them out of my head and finally drifted off

Now You See It, Now You Don't

The next day, Ryan and I walked back to the apartment after a hard day of work and class; dinner, a movie, and maybe a round of video games is what we had planned for that night. But, when we walked up the stairs to the 3rd floor, we reached my apartment with the number 306 on a silver plate fixed to the dark brown door already open. The inside of my apartment was not the same as when I left it in the morning.

My heart jumped as I pushed open the door with my foot: it should have been locked but it swung open freely. The living room was a wreck: clothes were strewn all over the floor, all our cabinet doors were open, couch pillows were everywhere. Was this really my apartment? Who would do something like this? I looked around the apartment and a dark cloud of anger came over me,

"I'll call the police." Replied Ryan, taking his phone out of his pocket. The muscles in his forearm stretched as he dialed.

* * *

As the police left my apartment, relief washed over me. One

officer turned towards me with a stern look and said,

"Please let us know if you need anything, madam..."

"Thank you, officer, it doesn't look like anything is missing," I replied with apprehension.

"I will call you if I need anything."

I nervously walked around the apartment, trying to figure out where I should begin cleaning up the mess that had been caused by their searching for evidence. My fear of someone always watching me become more and more evident with each passing second but I couldn't think about that right now.

"Ryan, hey we will catch up later OK. I need to sort myself out..."

"Are you sure you don't need help cleaning up?" He asked with genuine concern in his voice.

"Ya... I'm OK. I just want to be alone at the moment. If that's OK?" He nodded his head in understanding.

I didn't want to tell him of the mysterious box from my mom's bedroom that I found earlier; not yet anyway. Taking a deep breath, I began picking up the pieces of my life once more.

"Alright... just be careful tonight and make sure you lock your door and for god's sake, please call if you need anything. OK..."

"Alright. I will"

Ryan left my apartment giving me one last glance when I closed the door behind him. His face filled with worry and concern as he left me alone. It took me nearly two hours to clean up the apartment, and then it took me another hour trying to figure out if anything was missing, but to my surprise, nothing was. Who would break into a place and not take anything? They had to have been looking for something, I thought.

After cleaning up the apartment, I sat for a minute to catch my breath and found myself thinking of the dream I had the night before. The sand burned between my toes while she spoke in whispers,

I got out of bed and walked to my computer which was living in exile on top of a dark brown desk I had brought from the store. I tried to look up the word, 'Awana' on the internet and within seconds, a search listing appeared on my computer screen. Awana seems like a nice place to go on vacation in normal circumstances. But today is about finding out what this country town has anything to do with me.

Awana is a giant statue in Garland, which has a blend of Tropical Splendor and rich cultural heritage. This country is enriched with golden sandy beaches and lovely mountains. The people of Garland are of Mayan descent and speak an ancient dialect that is lost to the current world. The history of this nation can be traced back over 2500 years.

I sat down in front of my microwave dinner and slowly ate it as it my dinner would slip away. Even though everyone calls me 'Kailie' I wonder if it was really my name, I have no one to ask since my foster parents are no longer alive. But there is only one place in the State of Ontario that would have any record of who I am. So I searched for the number of the local social services.

I saved the website that mentioned the phone number and wrote it down on my to-do list for the next day. This made me feel less frustrated and powerless over my past situation. Ryan hates it when I do that, he keeps telling me that it's such a bad habit but it helps me to think. But at the moment I hate how no amount of thinking is helping me remember my past.

NOW YOU SEE IT, NOW YOU DON'T

The Fearful Confidant

Back inside Jonathan's house, the imposing figure of Phillip stood in his office, trying to explain to him about his latest mission that had tragically failed. His 6-foot frame was decorated with bulging muscles; a telltale sign of someone who had been hardened by military service. He wasn't wearing the typical uniform of the men he used to command, but instead was clad in fitting black pants, a T-shirt and a leather jacket. On his face was an intense look, one which spoke of a man near breaking point from his inner turmoil.

Phillip had been working for Jonathan for over five years, and despite the fear that he felt towards him, he confided in him and considered him his number one confidant. Yet, no amount of loyalty could protect him from his superiors' wrath.

"Sss... Sir. It wasn't there," stammered Phillip nervously.

"You failed me, Phillip." came the cold reply from Jonathan.

"Sir. I obeyed all the instructions you gave me..." pleaded Phillip desperately.

"I don't care if you followed the instructions," growled John, "What I wanted was the key. Don't make me do what I did to others." The room descended into oppressive silence as Jonathan stood up from his chair made of elephant hide, stretching out his short arms as he did so before turning to face Phillip squarely. His hands trembled as he reached into his pockets and pulled out a phone, dropping it nervously into Jonathan's hand like a fallen soldier surrendering their sword at the end of a battle.

"No sir," gulped Phillip, "I won't fail you again." His words hung heavy in the air as it dawned on Phillip that he had gone from being successful to failing at an alarming pace due to his father figure's threats. Now it seemed inevitable that he would be paying for it.

The Path to Your Past

I woke the following morning with a niggling feeling that something was going to happen. I remembered a dream from the previous night in which an older woman and a little girl were sitting on some flat surface reading an old book, in a language much different from English.

I woke up confused with the turbulence of thoughts in my head. Somehow in my dream, I understood the foreign language, but as I woke up I couldn't remember a thing. Why is this dream different from the previous one? This confused me.

"Something is going to happen, someone is calling me, I could feel that in every fiber in of body... I have to find out."

I laid back on my bed, anxious for 8 am to arrive. A few hours later, I jumped out of bed when the clock sounded its chirping alarm. I reached for the phone that was placed on by nightstand and dialed the number to the social service department.

"Hello this is Mike Fisher from social service. How may I help you?" said a voice from the other end.

"Hi, I am trying to find some information. My foster parent's name is Logan, and my name is Kailie, please tell me if there are any files about me on your computer."

"Please hold madam" replied Mike over the phone.

I was on hold with a customer service representative and starting to get anxious. I had been waiting for over ten minutes and my patience was wearing thin. The muzak playing in the background seemed to be interminable; I had started singing along to it without being aware. "Tan-data Adam dad-am da..." I hummed the tune absentmindedly, trying to fill the silence that seemed to have no end.

My boredom had quickly transitioned into anxiety, though it hadn't helped me get out of the situation any faster. I hadn't noticed how restless I was until I noticed my hair had almost entirely fallen out of the tight twist I had done it up in. Unconsciously, my fingers had started twirling strands of my hair around my finger like a lasso, an unconscious habit I had picked up to alleviate my anxiousness.

"Hi madam, thank you for holding. Yes, there is a file under Mr. and Mrs. Logan. But unfortunately, I can't give you any more information over the phone, you need to present me with a picture ID of yourself for security purposes."

"That's fine, I am going to come down to the office, how late are you open, today is a Sunday."

"We're open until 4 pm madam," came the reply.

"OK thank you"

"Your welcome, thanks for calling Toronto Social Services, have a nice day..."

* * *

The bright, sunlit streets of Toronto were almost black as I stepped out of my apartment building and closed the door behind me. The cold air froze my nose, even inside my jacket.

My breath was smoke in front of me as I inhaled through my mouth. It came in white puffs that disappeared into the freezing sky. I pulled down my hat over her ears, tucked my hands inside my jacket pockets, and started walking towards the social service as fast as my legs could carry me.

In the middle of the city of Toronto, was a tall yellow building that had the nameplate "Social Services" embossed on the wall. Inside the office was a small reception area in front and behind it was the employee's work cubicles which were separated by a glass. Wow, this is where all the lonely and lost kids come hoping for a family. How many of them actually get one, in that sense I was so lucky to have found my parents who loved me unconditionally. I walked towards the young girl at the reception who had a name tag, "Brenda".

"Hello madam, how can I help you," asked Brenda

"Yes, I am looking for Mike Fisher. I called in this morning.... He is expecting me."

"Please take a seat madam, and he will be right with you" replied Brenda

"Thank you"

I walked towards the brown chair that was placed horizontally along the wall next to the reception desk. Momentarily, a gentleman walked through the door from behind the reception. He had dark hair and tan skin. His jaw line was angular and smooth and completed the rest of his face, which had a pleasing masculine symmetry. He was wearing black pants, a white shirt with a blue tie.

"His strong voice said ''K... Kailie' said Mike

"Yeah that's me" I replied like a child excited to get candy

"Hi, my name is Mike"

"Hi, nice to meet you"

"Nice to meet you too, Please follow me, Miss."

I trailed him through the working cubicles. Most of the employee desks were filled with files in the "work in progress" section. There were some with their snacks on their tables, munching on them while they worked. Some were yelling on their phones and some were with foster families helping them adopt. Each of these files contained a name of a child, and I was one of them.

The Department for Children and Family Services looked like a marketplace, busy and loud. Mike's office was on the far right-hand corner of the building and inside the office were a large black leather chair and a nice view of the city of Toronto. It seemed like a different world inside this office. Everything was up-to-date and clean. Everything was in its rightful place. He even had a place for his pencil. I guess this is why he is a manager; organized, methodical, and a lot of experience.

"All the information about you is in here and even more. Please take a seat, Kailie." Said, Mike. Kailie looked at Mr. Fisher confused. But, managed to spit out the sentence,

"What do you mean even more..."

Calculating the Prophecy

The two priests, dressed in yellow robes, bent over the map laid out on the floor of their temple living room, studying it in silence. The map did not contain the land mass of Earth, as one might expect, but rather a map of nine planets arranged in an irregular fashion. Thousands of miles away from Kailie, the two priests could never have guessed how their work would shape the future of the world.

The priests had spent years poring over ancient manuscripts, searching for the key that would unlock the mysteries of the map. They had scoured religious texts, consulted with scholars, and even visited seers, all in the pursuit of knowledge.

Finally, they believed they had found the solution, and slowly, carefully, they outlined the nine planets with a finger, their eyes sparkling with excitement. They discussed in hushed tones the implications of their discovery, and finally, after a brief silence, one of the priests gestured to the map and declared, "This is the path to salvation."

It was the day that marked the beginning of the world's first interplanetary space exploration mission. The temple's discovery had unlocked the secrets of the cosmos, and now, with the help of their newfound knowledge, mankind could look to the stars for answers.

The older priest's hands shook as he carefully drew a circle around every written reference to the ruins. His pencil trembled in his grasp, leaving smudges and smears on the crinkled paper. He paused for a moment, then shook his head and put down his pencil.

"This can't be," said the old priest, his voice low and strained with worry.

The younger priest looked up at him incredulously. "What is it?" he asked, concern etched deep into his features.

"According to my calculations," the old priest said slowly, "the planets are placed here this year. Look at what the lines made." He gestured towards the diagram on the piece of parchment before them – a series of intersecting lines that formed a perfect pentagram.

"It's a pentagram. It's happening this year, isn't it?" The young priest's eyes widened in disbelief as he looked from his mentor to the ominous design on the page.

"I am afraid there is nothing much we can do except connect the dots." The old priest's tone was grim as he spoke. "This means she should be having her premonitions now." He turned to the younger man and held out a hand. "Pass me that phone, child."

As the younger priest reluctantly handed over his cell phone, an icy chill ran down his spine. Something terrible was coming, something beyond their understanding or control.

Snatch and Grab

In the mid-afternoon on a cold Toronto day, Ryan was trudging along the street. He could feel the chill of winter in the air and heard the low humming of an approaching vehicle. Suddenly, out of nowhere, a white van screeched to a halt beside him. Two menacing figures dressed in black with guns drawn leapt from the van and ran towards Ryan, yanking him off his feet and throwing him into the back seat like a rag doll. It happened so quickly that he couldn't react. His heart pounded against his ribcage as fear seeped through every pore of his body; would this be it? Would this be his last moment on Earth? Would he ever see Kailie again? The two masked men climbed into the front seat and drove Eighty-three kilometers north.

"Who are you? What's going on?" yelled Ryan while trying to free himself.

His shouts echoed reverberated throughout the van but no response came. The van eventually came to a complete stop and the men dragged him out, through the rain-drenched alleyway, and into an old door labeled "Warehouse 4". His mind raced as he slowly stepped inside; what awaited him within? Ryan sat in an ancient chair with bare wood and no cushion—he could feel its age within his bones as his fingers touched the wood beneath him. Fearful of what was coming next, he prayed silently for some kind of miracle.

The silence that filled the air was oppressive and almost suffocating as Ryan stood blinded by a black bag and bound tightly at the wrists. Sweat trickled down his forehead as he waited impatiently for what seemed an eternity, the only sound he could discern was the faint hum of the air conditioner. After several minutes he heard a familiar voice behind,

"You are going to help me one way or the other." And that was when he ceased all movement. He knew without a doubt who was behind those words and, for a brief moment, he felt lost, confused, and scared.

There was a shuffling sound and finally silence; then the bag was ripped off his head. Before him stood Jonathan James looking just as he always had—strangely pleasant but cold— and Ryan said nothing as he regarded his captor, who wore a sinister smile. As the seconds ticked by, Ryan broke the silence.

"Dad!" he exclaimed, his voice tinged with surprise and fear.

Begging For a Glimps

Some point of the day, Ryan was let go. Dumped like a bag of trash out the moving van. He walked to the end of the block, hopped over a phone book and stepped up onto the sidewalk. He didn't go to the cops or retaliate against his father. His body swayed slightly from side-to-side and forward to back as he walked towards Madam Theresa's store on the corner.

He looked down at this phone while standing beside the charm counter waiting for Madam Theresa. The screen was lit up with seven missed calls, all from Kailie. He pushed the button to put it on silent and slid it back into his pocket. Ryan has never been so scared but he has to find answers. The smell of incense, sage and candle wax wafted through the shop and a soft rumble came from beyond the velvet curtains that served as a doorway to another world.

"You again... I thought I had told you never to come here again." Walking out of the front room onto the porch, Madam T eyed him suspiciously and crossed her arms over her ample chest. Ryan met her gaze, willing himself not to look away. He needed information about Iris. Desperately.

"Please tell me.... What did you see? Please, I need to find a way to save her." he murmured, his words spilling out before he could stop himself. But Madam T had said no more than once and Ryan was driven out of the store and the door slammed behind him.

Ryan took a few deep breaths, trying to collect his thoughts. He had to find a way to get back in there, to understand what the gypsy lady had seen. He had to find a way to help Kailie.

His mind raced with possibilities as he tried to think of any way he could gain access to the store. He had to get the answers he needed – and he was determined to do whatever it took.

Items In The Box

Back inside the social service office, Mike gave me a box marked TSS on all four sides for Toronto Social Service. The box was old, the top flaps sealed shut with red tape and curled at the edges where it had been opened before and it smells musty, like old books or papers kept in a basement too long.

"Why wasn't this given to my foster parents who adopted me?" I asked, fingering the rough cardboard that prickled like thorns beneath my fingers.

"I have no idea, but there is nothing in the system about it either" Mike said.

My hands trembled as I opened the box and revealed its contents: a plush toy, two books, and a picture of a family. As my eyes settled on the photograph, I was sure that the little girl in the image and the one from my dreams were one and the same. A surge of emotion overwhelmed me and tears streamed down my face. My heart raced as a chill of anticipation and hope electrified me, bringing to mind memories of playtime with my brother and my loving parents.

My fingers trace over a forgotten toy that had been hidden within the shadows of time. Its fabric is worn and frayed, its once vibrant colors now dulled with disuse. How could I forget my brother? My mind shudders in horror as I recall all those years I had neglected such a precious memory. And yet here it was, an ever-present reminder of what I had lost.

Suddenly, I was transported back to my childhood, to days spent playing in the sunshine with "Jimmy," as I called it. I remembered how I used to talk to that toy as if it were alive. My eyes wandered across the box, and there they were - two books lying side by side. One was just a tattered old novel, but the other was something more special to me. It needed a key to open. The cover was torn at the edges and rain-soaked lines streaked its surface like veins running through skin. The pages inside were yellowed and brittle yet still held their magic intact- stories of far-off lands, exotic creatures, and ancient civilizations lost to time. As I opened the book that felt so old that the smell of aged parchment filled my nostrils and teased my nose hairs while my eyes darted greedily across each word.

"Where is the key Mike"

"What key!!" said Mike rifling through her box himself

"The key to this book, it has a lock."

"No madam there is no key, these are the only things that were in this box," replied Mike, looking through his computer log

She was disappointed now and let out a breath like she had been holding forever.

"More secrets...How come I wasn't remembering any of this before."

"Sometimes you need something dear to you to unlock your mind."

"I suppose.... OK... thanks, can I take this stuff home..."

"Yes, you may. But before you do, I have some paperwork I

need you to sign."

He turned to get them but I couldn't stop staring at the picture. How could someone so lovely be dead? And why just me who could see her? That woman. The woman in my dreams. She's my mom.

Secrets Revealed

I went to work that evening with a heavy load on my mind. I still hadn't told Ryan all that I had found or how I felt about him or my latest dreams. I looked like a person who had just lost her dog, or at least lost anything she ever loved, standing at the edge of an endless space filled with nothingness. The restaurant had no more than 15 people. It was about the right amount of people, considering it wasn't rush hour. I wiped down the middle table and pulled out the half-eaten plates left behind by the customer. They were the remains of potato skins and steak tips drowned in red sauce.

"This is a good day. A solid ten dollar tip. Not bad", I told myself as I slipped the few bills into my pocket on my black apron.

"Hey... how are you doing today...." said Ryan as she approached me with her notepad and pen in hand. He stood just out of reach. Even though we were surrounded by other employees and customers I smiled at him.

"I'm OK, just a little tired, that's all. I responded.

How long are you working till?" Ryan asked.

"Till 5, how about you?"

"I work till 5 too. And there is something I need to show you." replied Ryan, who was now taking orders for spaghetti.

"Sure... I have something to tell you too." I said continuing to clear tables and placing dirty dishes into the sink before heading home to shower and meet Ryan back at my apartment.

* * *

I opened the door to my small apartment, revealing the invited visitor. He was out of breath, his chest heaving with exertion, and as I took in the sight of him I felt a strange jolt of recognition — though, I couldn't explain why.

"What's wrong with you?" I asked, with an arched eyebrow.

"I ran," he replied between breaths. The words tumbled from his mouth as if he had been running for hours, and I couldn't help but be intrigued.

"Why were you running?" I asked suspiciously.

He shrugged, then took a moment to catch his breath. "No reason," he replied, and he seemed to be telling the truth.

I paused for a moment, considering what to do. Puzzled, but curious, I finally nodded and said, "Oooookkk come on in..."

Impatience had overcome me by the time Ryan arrived, and I had carelessly strewn everything across the bed - my mom's belongings, a few items from social services, and all of my own scattered possessions. Papers fluttered in the wind of the open window, while clothes lay in tangles around the room like exhausted marathon runners. The sheer chaos of it all made me feel overwhelmed. Finally, Ryan showed up and caught his breath at the sight.

"Here's the stuff"

As soon as I gave him the box, I noticed something written on the back of the picture. It said "Kailie Mia Wills"

Ryan's hand brushed against mine and our eyes locked. Mine showed surprise, his showed concern. This is not the first time he held my hand, but for some reason this time it felt different., but I ignored it.

"What..." Ryan replied softly, Ryan had always liked Kailie more than a friend, as she held her hand at that moment he felt his heart skip a beat. But he also knew with his father's plan, it is not the right time. So he looked away from Kailie before he couldn't stop controlling his feelings.

"See this little girl in the picture"

"Yeah," said Ryan, clearing his throat

"That's me, see this name at the back of the picture well that's my name...... Kailie Mia Wills, that's my real name and I have a brother too....... Adam.... How did I not see the back of the picture before."

"That's just awesome. Wait I'm going to check the internet, OK"

"Check the Internet for what."

"Something... Anything... Haven't you ever searched for your-self?"

"No Not really... Hmmm... never thought of that." I said and looked over Ryan's shoulder while he was typing on the computer keyboard.

Ryan typed the words 'Kailie Wills', and several sites pulled up. One, in particular, had a picture of a little girl. The same girl in my dreams and in the old picture. The girl on the computer had the same birthmarks as I did, her picture said missing, if found please contact 6725041525 and there was an address at the bottom.

Ryan didn't hesitate a minute to write the address down,

which eventually made him turn towards me. I looked at Ryan, kiss or not to kiss is the question I had at that moment. I wanted to kiss him but I didn't know how he would react to it. I don't want to lose my best friend if he doesn't like me back. My heart was raising but I had to suppress my feelings, yet I kept looking into his eyes. Everything else around me became irrelevant and he shifted slightly in his chair. I took a step back, to give him his space and turned around. As soon as I turned, he grabbed my hand and stood up. He looked at me with those perfect eyes that melted my heart. Before even I knew what was happening, he leaned in and placed a gently wet kiss on my lips, igniting a fire within me that fueled my every move. He pulled back, concern etched across his face, wondering if he had made the right decision. But I felt his breath on my lips as I fought to make sense of everything. Then, in an instant, I kissed him back with an intensity I didn't know existed within me. We slowly moved apart from each other – our hands still entwined – and took a deep breath before finally breaking into a smile. The world around us seemed brighter and full of possibility.

"Hi," I said.

"Hi" he replied, holding my hands with a smile then he cleared his throat and glanced back at the computer screen that showed the address.

"Looks like we are going to Garland." said Ryan

"We are? Why?...." I replied softly, as I was still having butterflies from my previous encounter with Ryan

"Are we not going to talk about what just happened?" I asked, and waited for his reply which consisted of just a smile, but then managed to say

"Kailie, I love you.. I have wanted to kiss you since the first day I met you.. If you don't feel the same way you need to tell me now"

"Is this what you wanted to tell me"

"Maybe," he said with a smile on his face

"Ryan, I would be lying, if I say I don't feel the same way too. But I have to focus on this right now. Is that OK with you"

Ryan reached for my hand, gently placed it in his and leaned over to kiss me again. My heart skipped a beat as I melted into the kiss. He was so good at this. His lips were warm soft and full, like I'd imagined they would be. He pulled away and smiled at me.

"We can do both right?"

I nodded and smiled back at him wondering where all of this would lead.

He squeezed my hand and from the look in his eyes I knew he didn't have any regrets about making love to me either. With that knowledge came a giddy excitement as I realized we had taken another step forward together, whatever came next.

"OK.. now that we got that out of the way, Kailie, what if your brother is still alive, don't you want to know who you really are, what if it's the answer to all your dreams and your parents, I mean your biological parents. What are you destined for and most of all what are you supposed to save, what is this legend... don't you want to know all these things"

"Ya but what does Garland have to do with anything..." I asked

"Because the internet said so..."

"Oh OK... but all these things are a bit too much to handle right now..."

"I know that Kailie, but this is something you have to do, Summer holidays are coming, so school is out for 3 months, it's a perfect time," said Ryan giving me a quick hug and a kiss on my forehead.

Ryan turned back towards the computer and started to read more, while I sat on the bed playing with the soft toy that was inside the box. A smile swapped across my face as I remembered the intimate memories I had of that animal. However, my eyes shifted to another item that built my curiosity. It was the book that had a lock on it. The design on the cover looked very familiar. The four designs on the four corners and its antique look got her mesmerized. Then my eyes glanced at another item, it was the box I got from my mom's closet.

"Ryan, It's the same... the design is the same... how did something in the same design go to my foster parents and also in this box. That box mom stored my stuff in her room would have been mine." I said holding both items in her hand.

"But, I can't figure out how to open this book, but look... this box and the book has the same design and the box came from my foster mom and this book from the orphanage."

"Let me see.... How did you open the box? Maybe it's the same way to open the book."

"No, it can't be... look at this keyhole in the book. it's almost like a star..."

"Kailie this inscription looks awfully familiar to me"

Ryan worked his fingers through the book design that was engraved on a bronze metal and pasted on the book. I reached out to see the inscription and suddenly Ryan's eyes glanced at my neck. Is he going to kiss me again? Nothing is going to get done if I keep kissing him, even if I really want to. His strong arms reached for the necklace and it accidentally became visible through my t. shirt.

"Oh my god, Kailie, It's been under your nose this whole time."

"What is."

"The Key... silly. Take off your necklace. I'll show you. It's your charm. Your necklace is the key."

I took the chain out of my neck and placed it on the lock. As soon as I placed it, the metal flaps on the book opened. Ryan and I looked at each other with surprise and anxiety to know what the book enclosed. They gently opened the cover.

The book was filled with information but it was in a different language, and such knowledge of that language is no longer known to me. But there were few words written in English, "Tallest statue, Awana, Garland. Priest Taho"

Thoughts

As the hot water cascaded down his body, droplets of steam hung in the air like tiny clouds. Ryan emerged from the shower, his slim 6-pack waist wrapped with a white towel, while taking his hand through his wet hair he laid down on the bed thinking about Kailie. The sound of rain tapping against the window filled the room as Ryan's thoughts wandered to the image of Kailie twirling in a lovely yellow and white dress, her hair flowing behind her like strands of gold. He imagined her dancing to the soft music under the moonlight, surrounded by a garden of blooming flowers and scents of jasmine.

Ryan out of his daydream and back in reality answered the phone with excitement hoping it would be Kailie

"Hello ...."

"Hello..." replied the voice from the other end of the phone, making Ryan tremble in fear.

"Dad!!!"

"You are supposed to do something for me, son..."

Ryan's heart pounded in his chest as he stammered,

"Da - a - dad. I don't want to do this. I am not going to be a part of your bidding, Dad." The silence on the other end of the cordless phone was deafening before his father spoke again.

"Is that so... Ryan..." His voice was cold and menacing.

"You get your head out of your ass, son. This is what I have been training you for. I am going to get it either way. If you don't want me to kill everyone you have ever loved, including your mother and sister, I suggest you do what I tell you to do."

The weight of fear threatened to crush Ryan's soul. His mind raced as he thought about how much he had missed his mother and sister since they had been taken away from him all those years ago when Jonathan and Ryan's mother divorced when he was just five. What could he do now?

"Yes sir," replied Ryan, his voice small and subservient. He couldn't let anything happen to the only family he had left.

Jonathan hung up, leaving Ryan alone with his thoughts. He tried to push back the tears that threatened to spill over but found himself unable to hold them back any longer.

He pressed the "off" button on his cordless phone and went into deep thought, haunted by memories of his past and fears for his future. Then the phone rang again.

The jarring ringtone broke through the stillness of the room like breaking glass. Ryan jumped in surprise before picking up the phone once more.

"Hello." His voice trembled with fear as he thought it was his father calling him again.

"Hi it's me Kailie... are you alright..." Her voice was soft and velvety, calming Ryan like a warm blanket on a cold night.

"Hi. Ya ya. I'm alright... I was just thinking about you"

"oh ya.. me too. Hey, I just wanted to say thanks, for everything. You have always been there for me."

"Of course, anything for you." He smiled and relaxed into his chair realizing that all would be okay if she were there with him in the room.

"Well good night" I replied softly

He tried hard to say something else, but found more diffi-culty speaking now than he had before when his father was threatening him. He sat there holding his phone, thinking about the previous phone call and how she had saved him from that situation. The only way he could think of returning that favor was to say something else, but he didn't know what it should be.

The Travel

The next morning, our journey began at the Toronto Airport. The flight to Garland took the better part of a day; from Toronto via Tokyo and Singapore sounded more like a journey into space than across an ocean. We landed in Garland around 8 am and rented a car from the airport itself and drove ahead to a city that looked nothing like the area where the airport was. This place had tall buildings and friendly people; the country was surrounded by lovely golden sandy beaches that stretched into the horizon like a painting come to life.

In 45 minutes we reached a tall building overlooking a sandy beach, with heavy guns lining its walls from long ago when Garland fought battles against other countries. A garden full of flowers and beautifully designed stone walkways sloped gently down toward the shoreline.

Ryan and I entered the hotel through the large parking lot. A tower of glass doors opened into a lobby, lit by chandeliers and filled with white leather sofas, burgundy armchairs, and gold-framed paintings of ships on the ocean. There was already a cluster of guests there, standing around like we were waiting for someone to close our eyes and paint us in their sketch pad.

An older man in a burgundy jacket walked around offering juice made from scratch that was poured from an insulated pitcher. He had already served all the guests standing around who had just arrived, and now began walking towards us.

"Thank you, " we said while reaching for our glasses.

Ryan picked up his backpack and was on his way toward the reception, which would be bustling with employees handling the different tasks like taking care of reservations and handling day-to-day operations that keep a hotel running smoothly.

Ryan reached over the counter separating guests from the employees to talk to the receptionist who just hung up the phone after speaking with another customer. Reaching over the grenade counter,

"Hi, I reserved a room on the Internet. Here is the conformation mail I got"

"Thank you, sir, please give me a minute to check our system"

"Here you go sir, your room number is 728 one of our employees will follow you to your room with the bags. Hope you enjoy your stay here"

"Thanks"

On the seventh floor, I followed one of the employees Gwen through the off-white painted walls illuminated by the bright lights. It led us to our bedroom, where two beds covered in crisp white sheets stood at either side overlooking the endless ocean. The smooth breeze rolling in from outside always smells like saltwater and sand.

"Wow," I said, my voice trembling with the effort of taking in the room. "This place is beautiful." I turned my head sweeping my hair off her face, and from the corner of my eye, I saw Ryan stare.

"What... why are you staring at me"

" No... no reason..... no reason at all" as he walked towards me and and smiled as he reached for my hand and pulled me close. I turned to face him, and before I saw anything else, his lips locked on mine. He kissed me tenderly, and I felt myself melting under his touch.

"You look beautiful"

"So what are the clues we have," said Ryan switching gears.

I collapsed onto the bed with her arms up over her head. "Well, I know we have to be at a place called Awana, and meet a priest name Taho... But can we please rest a bit? My feet hurt like hell."

The Temple of Awakening

The next day, after breakfast, Ryan and I drove to Awana. The small town was 6 hours North from where we were. We drove past the different landscapes from the beachfront to low land in a few hours and then a beautiful area of hills and cold weather.

The air here hit my face like a cold slap when we stepped over the threshold. For a few minutes I couldn't catch my breath as I took in this wide, fresh space. We were about to leave the main city behind. Not too long after, we reached the dry area with miles and miles of paddy fields. The harvested rice had been put away to keep out hungry animals, and it all looked golden and ready for new seedlings. Ancient kingdoms and pillars that once supported the large structures of monasteries and palaces were left ruined on the floor, with uncontrollable weeds on top of it claiming their new territory, forcefully grabbing the pillars towards nature. Although there was no more glory or royal line here to rule this land, one could see—as if it was still standing in its full majesty—a grand structure that might have been a palace or a temple. Very disturbing though, was the fact that these old ruins now housed spirits roaming at night.

We have now reached our destination - the rural town of

Garland. The gentle rolling hills were covered in an unbroken blanket of fresh green grass, as far as the eye could see. There was so much to see, so much to visit. It was a nice little mini vacation with Ryan, even though we only started dating very recently, I have known him all my life and it was nice to get away from our everyday life. We may need another vacation after this but at least we started somewhere.

As we arrived at Awana, the crunching of our tires on the gravel lot was the only sound in the air. We stepped out of the car and began to make our way towards the staircase carved out of the long-standing rock. The steps were narrow and steep, with jagged edges that looked like they could slice through skin like butter if one wasn't careful. Sweat was already starting to form on my forehead as I concentrated on where I was placing each foot, fearful of falling down the rocky steps below.

On top of the uneven stairway was a passage of rocks that had stood for centuries. Back in its prime, it would have looked like a tall wall, but age had weathered it down and caused it to crumble and fall in some places. At the entrance of this ancient structure, two small rocks were carved in the shape of a snake, marking our destination as clear as day.

And finally, we saw it. It was a key element of Garland's history - an imposing structure that had witnessed countless generations come and go. The sheer size of it was awe-inspiring; it was almost as if time itself had stopped while standing before it.

As we approached, I felt a sense of reverence wash over me - one that can only be summoned when standing in front of something truly grand.

The stone statue of Awana was a man in the standing posture on a lotus platform, arms and legs posed like a dancer. An unknown sculptor had carved the warrior from granite during ancient times. A large oil lamp made out of rock sat at his feet. The once-standing roof had perished, leaving debris scattered around the statue. It had stood for centuries through rain and storm and war. The air smelled of incense and pollen, carried with the draft into the shrine room.

To my right was an enormous bow tree, its leafs swaying to the light wind giving it a calm sound. A local group of tourists offered flowers to the tree and said their prayers. They were all dressed in white down to the 2-year-old girl who was with them. It appeared to be out of respect to wear long, light-colored clothing when visiting this place. Near the Awana statue was another group of tourists taking pictures, documenting their visit. A little further behind the bow tree was a hut that extended in a semicircle around the trunk, and by now I saw a young priest wearing orange robes walking toward us from the direction of the temple.

"Are you looking for someone?"

I put my hands together, as I learned it was a sign of respect. "Yes, my name is Kailie... and ..." before I could finish my sentence.

"Priest Taho has been expecting you, please come with me"

I looked at Ryan in surprise. "How do they know I would be here.... I have a weird feeling about this. He knew me..."

"Well it's about time someone did..." replied Ryan.

We followed the young priest inside the hut, which was full of statues of Buddha, warriors, and Kings. The lighting in the hut was dim yellow, which made everything in that room radiate and glow.

Our footsteps echoed on the stone floor as we walked to the center of the room. A table spread with tea cups, cookies, and other treats filled its expanse.

The priest smiled broadly at us and motioned towards us to sit on small silk pillows that were scattered over the floor.

"Good morning," Priest Taho said when we had both settled onto our pillows. A deep smile seemed to light up his eyes; they were shaped like almonds framed by a serene face that exuded wisdom, compassion, and joy.

"I have been waiting for you."

"Do you know who I am?" I asked.

He shook his head at my question but kept smiling. "Oh yes we have met before! But you were not this tall last time I saw you..."

The Message

A lightning storm raged across the night sky. Jonathan stood in his expansive study with his back to the bay window and watched as flashes of light tore through the blackness. He fumbled around in his pockets before finding his phone which was vibrating incessantly.

For a moment, everything was silent except for the howling wind outside. The sounds of nature seemed starkly out of place with the modern feel of the room. A bright lamp blazed on one end of a massive mahogany desk, while a dark leather couch lined one wall opposite two floor-to-ceiling bookcases.

"Garland is it? Wonderful... You will do exactly what I say, understand Ryan?"

Jonathan heard a newfound steel and determination in his son's voice,

"This is it Dad... I am done. If you lay a hand on my mother or sister, so help me God... I will kill you myself!" Ryan paused for a moment before asking in a soft whisper, "Did you ever love us?"

Jonathan was silent for a few moments before icily replying "Love has nothing to do with this. It's all about power" before abruptly ending the call.

The History Lesson

"You are the savior of all living things, the last hope for all humanity."

I was starting to get annoyed with priest Taho as he didn't give me a proper answer. Everything he said sounded like it was coming out of a fortune cookie and I had questions. The same words all came back at me, sawing away in my ear like a dopey mantra: Forgiveness... acceptance... future... After the fifth time, I'd had enough. I tried hard not to appear rude to the priest. But the look on my face would have given it away.

"Ya, sorry... I don't know what that means..." I blurted out

While pointing towards the star shaped pendant around my neck, the priest replies,

"The small, round charm you have on your neck is the key to finding everything. Your past and your future, you are the single most powerful creature on earth. A long time ago, a king named King Tomka found a crystal that had great power, but the crystal's power was too great for one person to handle. King Tomka knew that, but he kept it a secret from his brother, Telkish, who wanted the power of the crystal to rule the kingdom as he wasn't given the throne after his father's death.

One of King Tomka's trusted advisors gave all information regarding the crystal to Telkish who used the guard to retrieve the crystal. At the time of the alignment, the crystal picked greed and evil over good and light, and all living things died. The land died of hunger and plague; light turned into dark on earth, and all people died of sickness and famine. King Tomka ran away in shame and disbelief.

As time crept forward, King Tomka returned with an army to battle with his brother Telkish. Each night and day ended with blood and pain. Mountains of bodies piled up by the river bed. The battles raged on for 18 years, during which many people were wounded while others perished in rival's swords and last-ditch curses. Yet King Tomka did not give up. One fateful night when King Tomka was killed in battle by Telkish, he used his last dying breath to say an incantation over a gem which glowed bright as a star. At that moment, he vowed that the crystal can only be activated with the blood of his line. The God's granted that request by making the king's only daughter "Sophie" the guardian of that place. When King Tomka was killed in battle by Telkish, he used his last dying breath to say an incantation over a gem which glowed bright as a star. But Telkish yelled out another spell just before his blade pierced King Tomka's chest. The two brothers were both saying different incantations at the same time to gain power, the crystal consumed Sophie and went to sleep for 5000 years. Before the great battle, Princess Sophie had given a key shaped like a heart to her 2-year-old daughter, who was taken away by a maid of the castle to protect her and raise her as her own. The legends say that you need to discover this key within yourself if you wish to wake up the spirit hidden within the temple.

But in 5000 years, when the crystal's power awakens, it would choose to use its powers for good or evil. If it chose the darkness then Princess Sophie's soul would remain trapped there forever. Our job was to make sure that happened and destroy the crystal. You were her great great great granddaughter, but such knowledge of the ancient Garland language had been lost. It was said that this temple was alive somehow. For thousands of years people had tried to find the crystal, but every man who entered the temple had never returned. It was said that it was cursed.

"This wooden box is a family heirloom, an antique you received from your mother before her death. Kailie, you have been sent here to stop the greatest evil of all, the dark side that seeks to consume all that is light. You are our only hope for survival. Your mother left 16 years ago in search of the hidden inscription that holds the key to finding the crystal of salvation, yet she was slain before she could uncover it. Just before her last breath, she managed to hide the map with a cryptic engraving. We thought you had died with your mother until I discovered many years later that you were still alive."

The priest pointed at a grainy picture and began,

"This is the image of a crystal... and it.."

Kailie cut him off,

"Yes I remember that's the same crystal that my mother was holding in my dreams – one hand gripping the necklace and stretching towards the sky..."

He bowed his head in reverence.

"My child, your mother never found the crystal... what you saw was a mix of your past and future.

Before your mother was killed, she promised her soul would remain beside you till you uncovered its secrets. So she came to you in your dreams to show you what to do – how to use the necklace as a key to solve this puzzle and locate the crystal. Your mother never found the crystal herself; instead, she provided you with just enough clues so that you can put together the pieces and save us all."

The crystal, a sparkling gemstone the size of a man's fist, looked as though it had been carved from pure sunlight. Its raw power could be used for either great good or tremendous evil. The date was set, 12 midnight in 18 days when the sun, the earth, and the moon would align vertically with the other planets aligned around earth like a pentagram. At that exact moment, a portal would open. If evil stood on that particular spot, it would spread throughout the world like a malignant virus: light turning to dark and life twisting into death.

"You must complete what your mother started," the old priest said in a voice that crackled with age and urgency. "This portal only opens every 5000 years." His eyes glowed as he spoke, and his gnarled fingers clutched at the loose folds of his robe.

"Why a pentagram"

"The pentagram is a symbol of good magic before evil stole it."

"Why me and not my brother"

"It has to be the female line to carry on the power because women are the creator of life. The supreme being."

My head was in a tumult. I felt like a cork washed along the waves of an infinite ocean, rising and falling with the choppy swells, meandering on its journey without sense of purpose or direction. For so long I had toiled desperately, scavenging for scraps of data that would make sense of the unfolding events. Now it was all within reach. But could I comprehend it? What would be the outcome of this newfound knowledge? It was too much to bear. My questions chased one another with such rapidity - each answer unearthing three more queries in its wake.

"Is my father and brother still alive?" I braved to query, holding my breath as I awaited the response. The priest smiled kindly in reply, "Yes child, they are indeed."

My heart was overcome with joy and gratitude, everything seemed possible now but, I couldn't help but wonder. Why did they not come looking for me?.

Meet The Family

Back again through the carved stone staircase, I walked towards the hut. There were two gentlemen standing next to the younger priest. The closer I got to the hut, the more the two people were staring at me. One was a young man not more than 35 years old. He was wearing blue jeans and a white polo shirt. His dark brown hair curled in thick waves around his ears. He stood with his hands on his waist, looking proud but relaxed, like a sort of well-built superhero. The other gentleman seemed older, about 65 years old or so, with a head filled with silver-gray hair cut short and neatly trimmed. He wore neat cargo pants and a tee shirt printed with some kind of logo.

As I approached, the tears on the older gentleman's face became visible. My heart started to pound, and my breathing became shallower and more rapid. This was the moment I had been waiting for—the moment of reunion with my long-lost father. What do I do? How should I react? Ryan knew exactly what to do; he held my hand as a way of comforting me in contrast to my flustered state and let me know that he was there for me. The older gentleman took my hands in his own as if exploring an ancient treasure. He gradually touched my face with his right hand while maintaining eye contact as if seeking some lost secret contained within their depths.

"Father," I said softly.

"Yes." His eyes brimmed with an emotion that pierced me to my core.

I threw my arms around him in desperation, pulling him close with all the might I could muster. The scent of his cologne, a musky blend of jasmine and sandalwood, filled my senses as I held on tight. So many questions swirled through my mind like a tempestuous storm, but for now, this embrace was enough.

"Why didn't you come to see me after you found out I was alive? Where were you all this time? What happened to…."

"I was waiting for this moment for a long time," he replied softly, brushing his fingers through my hair as he spoke.

"But why didn't you contact me after the Priest found where I was three years ago?"

"Because you had to know about your destiny on your own and it was the only way to keep you safe."

"But…I was just a child and why…"

"Because you're the chosen one. The supreme being. And I only learned about you three years ago. Believe me, I wanted nothing more than to take the next flight to you, but I understood the importance of letting you figure it out on your own. I promised your mother"

I was still not satisfied with the answers I received, my heart burned with questions. But, I decided to just be happy that I found my long lost family.

I glanced over at the man standing beside him. "Hi…" he said, holding out his hand towards me.

"So that makes you my Big Brother," I said in response.

"Oh sorry, this my Ryan…I mean Ryan" I looked around for

help with embarrassment. Ryan stepped forward and smiled warmly, which was when I noticed how incredibly cute he was. "Her boyfriend Ryan," he finished with a wink in my direction, smoothing everything over.

The relief washed over me like a tidal wave when I saw that he had cleared out our relationship status, because I could never have done it myself. But despite my trepidation, the name "boyfriend" still sent a thrill down my spine every time I heard it. It was official now. I was his.

"Now that everyone has met, let's get started." said the priest.

Hidden Cave

After thirty minutes of hiking, and exploring the untouched path through the woods, the leaves were thick and green and looked alive despite being still. Every so often, they would stop moving in a breeze. At the ground level, we traveled single file on an unmarked path through the shrubbery behind the temple. It began to thin out as we approached a dip in the ground where an old building structure once stood. We started walking inside the cave, leading into a shadowy section of land where nothing grew. We passed by untold trees and bushes until we reached a fork in the tunnel where two paths split off from each other in opposing directions, and there was no light in sight. Then, all of sudden, we stopped. I wasn't sure what was going on, but I decided to roll with it and take it as it came.

"The necklace my child"

The Priest reaches his hand uncovering a deep burn mark on his wrist. The skin was raw, scabbed over in places, folded and twisted back onto itself like ashes, which was covered all this time. The light dimmed around me as if a cloud passed over the sun, and I squinted my eyes, trying to remember my life and death all those years ago. Flashbacks of my dream appeared in my head and I remembered why I lived when everyone else died so many years ago.

"It was you wasn't it?" I said looking at Priest Taho's arm.

Everyone looked at me puzzled

"You are the one who pulled me out of that cave. All those years ago... You saved my life.. It was you wasn't it... I recognize that scare."

"Yes, it was me. I brought you here. I told you to stay here because the village was under attack. But when I returned for you, You were gone."

"I went back... in search of Dad. I remember a river by a waterfall"

"That's a few KM that way" replied the priest

I reached for the necklace on my chest wondering what it was that the old priest held out towards me. He pressed the small, sharp-ended charm towards the indentation in the wall. The sound of thunder rang in my ears and shook through my body as if we were standing in a great hall somewhere amidst a storm. The stone slowly parted to reveal an opening cut into the side of the cave. A cool breeze blew from within its depths. Suddenly, I knew exactly where this passage would lead us.

Dense clouds of dust erupted through the open door, old and stale and drifting out into the air. It had been years since anyone had passed through the entranceway to this cave. The wisps of smoke twisted through the air like ethereal spirits dancing with the wind.

We pushed open the door and switched on the lights. I stood there stunned, not knowing what to say, but looked at Ryan in disbelief. For the first time, I was lost for words.

The room seemed like a museum exhibit: the items were placed carefully upright in glass display cases; each item sat gently illuminated by light from above as if it too needed the light to exist. Some of the items were military equipment: guns, grenades, knives, radios, GPS systems, linens... although they didn't have names or labels on them. There was also some clothing and household objects mixed in with the military gear: bowls and plates and clothes folded neatly into a dresser drawer. There was a child's toy box with stuffed animals and a wooden train set inside. A small desk held books about history, astronomy, science, archaeology, psychology, religion, novels... a place where someone could immerse themselves in science or just imagine an ordinary life. This was someone's treasure chest. On a flat rock at least two feet wide sat five metal boxes stacked like firewood facing out to fill the space of the stone shelf.

"Father, did you know about this... How did you manage to hide all this from... well, everyone..." I asked trying to understand the pieces of my past.

"No, he didn't know my child, and when you want to hide something and with a person whose mind is trained to never use it... That's why your mother only entrusted me with this secret." Said the priest

"We will start training at 6 in the morning. We have only 18 days and I want all 3 of you to be here by 6 am" said Father.

"Great.... I feel loved already" I said with a smirk on my face.

Day 17 - Training

I woke up the next morning to a world steaming with moisture.
The air was cold and thick, like cotton. Behind me nestled the
valley; in front of me—the forest. I hoped that my body heat
would be enough to keep me alert for another hour or two before
the sun rose. The dim white light crept through the canopy of
trees and flowed down onto the path. Each drop bounced off a
leaf and then landed on my face, making my eyes water. To my
right was Ryan's tent; to my left was Adam's; behind me was
my father's. Walking through the mist of morning air... Father,
yells,

"Alright, Kids. Out of the tents. Take a seat...."

Few minutes later, Ryan emerges from the tent, dressed and
ready to go. The smile he flashes me melts my heart. When he
approaches and gently kisses my cheek, I nearly buckle at the
knees. We take our seats on logs placed around a dead fire, and
father hands the boy's three steaming mugs of coffee.

"We have less than three weeks to accomplish what we need
to do," Dad announces.

"Kailie, you are our only hope. Your mother hid the map just
before she died. We have to find it and find the crystal before

the full moon. These few weeks will be hard work, but I know you guys can handle it. One thing is certain: Adam knows the route—eight miles through heavy underbrush with the last one on walking. Let's get running." He continued.

Adam, Ryan, and I begin jogging through thick woods; suddenly my eyes shifts to some unseen object to a different place in my mind. This time it is not a physical picture that flashes across my vision; instead an entirely mental image appears— a flashback of Mom running through these same woods as daylight fades into dusk.

"Kailie are you OK?" asked Ryan

"Ya, I am fine. let's go." I replied shaking off the mental image.

We ran up the hill, then down the hill, across the stream, and up the hill again. I had to keep myself from vomiting and leaned on thin air as my body moved without me. The forest was covered in a light blanket of fog. Up ahead were two figures. Father and the priest stood together under a large oak tree. I staggered through the last few meters of the run, stumbling toward them. They patted my back and smiled at me.

"We have to train you harder than this," said the priest.

I walked over to a nearby boulder, sat down, and fought against falling asleep. Punch this, punch that. I rolled onto my side but I could barely move my arm and even if I could, it wouldn't matter; they would just hit me again anyway. From martial arts to strengthening exercises to flexibility exercises followed by breaking boards into meditation and many more, which went on for several hours each day for several days. My legs were wobbly at first but soon enough they grew strong again.

* * *

The moon was high in the sky. The rocks surrounding the temple were bathed in silver, and their shadows cast monstrous structures that moved as the clouds drifted overhead. Several miles away from the temple a camp of 20 guards had been set up for the evening. Some of the guards set up tents. Some sharpened their weapons. Some laughed with one another while they worked. One guard stood apart, staring at a sleeping Jonathan James

"If my calculations are right, they should be right here." Said Jonathan

"Should we get ready Sir?" asked a guard

"No, Let's enjoy tonight. We break at dawn."

Day 9 – Time To Pack Up

When the priest opened the cave of armor again, my eyes lit up like bright stars, and my smile spread across my face until it was so big that it hurt; I could not contain the excitement and happiness welling up within me. Ryan and Adam were standing next to me as we waited for the priest.

"Children come with me," said the priest

"We are heading out tomorrow morning, so grab what you need," said Father

"Kailie take this. Put it somewhere that is safe." Replied the priest handing me a piece of paper.

The paper was old, discolored and the edges were worn out. Due to time it had become an almost indistinguishable yellow color. The content written on it was clear but made no sense to me. It had symbols and arrows, some with translated inscriptions on the side that I didn't understand. It was mom's handwriting.

"What is this..." I asked

"This is the map I told you about, a part of it - the first half of it. Your mother discovered the first half of the code and handed it to me in case something was to happen to her. She was on her way to crack some more of the code written on the map. But someone killed her before she could finish." replied the Priest.

"Are you sure I am the one? I am not sure if I can do this."

"Life is a blessing, my child. Live it. And you will only succeed when you have a little faith... This is your destiny." said the priest as he walked out. Although, I never understood his comments.

* * *

That night outside the tent, training wasn't the only thing that happened. The training was tough as usual, but getting closer and closer to judgment day was making me nervous and awake through the night. Crickets clattered outside my tent seemed louder than ever, the cold air seemed colder, and I tossed and turned until I was fully awake. I couldn't sleep. Dressed in my black and pink pajamas, I walked outside the tent. Glazing towards the endless lake, I suddenly heard the noise of light footsteps. The sound echoed off the wooded lake bank, floating into the starry sky like whispers of thieves trying to escape with their ill-gotten loot. I quickly turned around and there he was standing, staring right back at me.

"You can't sleep either ha..." asked Ryan walking towards me.

"No... a bit nervous I guess."

He stood behind me, hands reaching over my body alongside my shoulders, holding them close together. His lips brushed against my neck and continued to just hug me as I leaned back into him and let out a deep sigh.

I reached up and put my hand on his forearm, squeezing his fingers between mine. My lips quivered slightly, in need of a kiss. Our hearts beat in time with each other and we were alone, surrounded by trees. I closed my eyes and smiled at the thought of being alone with him.

"I love you," he whispered into my ear. I quickly turned around to face him, smiling.

"What?" I asked, shocked by his words.

"Sorry no that just came out. I mean..." Ryan started to brush off the slip-up by making it worse by trying to cover it up.

"I love you too.." I replied before he could finish stammering. He flashed a gentle smile and kissed me on the lips one time. Ryan let out a deep sigh but was stil smiling.

"Are you alright?" I asked while looking deeply in his eyes for some answers. He turned away from me and then looked back at me again slow as if troubled by something weighing heavily on his mind.

He picked up a twig from the ground and began to toy with it between his fingers as he spoke,

"Ya I am OK"

"Ahh Shit, who am I kidding. I'm lying, you know I'm lying.. I met my Dad, Kailie."

"Oh, that's great. is that why you were acting all weird." Asked Kailie

"He is a bad person, Kailie. He left my mom, sister, and me all those years ago and only contacted me recently because he wanted something. He wants me to do things I don't want to do... I don't want anything to do with him, he hurts people to get his way" said Ryan.

"Ryan. I'm sure you're exaggerating," replied Kailie

"You don't know him as I do, K. Anyway. I'm going to bed, I'll see you tomorrow, okay. get some sleep" said Ryan kissing my forehead before walking away.

"Good night," I replied, but I felt there was more and that he was not telling me everything. I waited till he walked out of my site and into his tent.

Day 7 – The Opening

Early morning the next day, Adam, Ryan, and I dressed appropriately and armed ourselves with weapons. The sun beat down against our armor; droplets of sweat ran down my neck while we waited outside the cave.

"Hey you ready to rock and roll," said Adam

"As cheesy as that sound... apparently I was born to do it..." said Kailie,

"That's even cheesier," said Ryan jokingly.

We headed out toward the unknown future with hope and strength. We drove north for a few hours. I had fallen asleep as it seemed like it would take us only five minutes, but when I opened my eyes; we had reached our destination.

We pulled off the cracked road and parked at the edge of a thicket on a small, sandy embankment. The trees' lower boughs hung high overhead. We started to walk through the forest, making our way between huge leafy ferns that shot up above my head like pillars in a cathedral. Some were so tall I couldn't see their tops and no sunlight filtered down. Halfway through the dark woods, I turned around to get my bearings but everything looked the same for miles and miles.

"I suppose we won't come back down the same route," I said sarcastically.

Few minutes later, we reached a point high up on top of a rock, and we could see everything below us — a sea of redwoods stretching out in every direction. The low sun was creeping to the horizon, lighting the tops of the trees like liquid gold. I was short of breath, flashes of memories coming in and out of my head. I saw my mom running, then in a flash, I saw how she died. I couldn't take another step; I collapsed to the floor, trying to catch my breath. Ryan ran towards me to help me up.

"Kailie what's wrong..." asked Ryan worried

"Mom.... I saw Mom" I replied, catching my breath.

Priest Taho turned towards Kailie stunned.

"My child, this is where we found your mother's body. The map should be somewhere here. It's not surprising how her soul is still connected to you."

While everyone was looking for a clue or a path of some kind, I started mattering to myself as if I was possessed.

"Kailie did you say something," asked Adam

"Ya, I ran this way and over here I was hiding. Then I walked about five more steps. There should be a cave. I hid there for 2 days" I replied while moving toward a large rock, covered with bushes and overgrown weeds. I pulled it to the side, and there was a flat, hard surface.

"This is it... I found it..."

I went inside to see if my intentions were right. The darkness surrounded me with a frigid embrace. I fumbled in the dark for my flashlight, which illuminated a path that led across the length of the cavern. My legs trembled, as my eyes adjusted to the milky light and I was riddled with uncertainty and doubt. As soon as I touched the cool stone beneath my feet, I knew what to do but could not explain why. The air smelled thickly of damp soil and stale water, like an old well or cellar.

"How do I open this?" I asked at the foot of the dead end.

"These caves and doors were made about 5000 years ago, during the times of our kings. We are under an old castle which is in ruins right now. There has to be some sort of thing that will trigger this door to open" said the priest

"Yes, that explains the carvings on the walls and the touch holders……. And…… the cobwebs…" said Adam while dusting the cobwebs from his hand.

The others immediately began to look for a way to open the hidden door. Ryan, however, leaned against the wall to drink some water. Suddenly, his gun knocked over and hit a small part of the wall. The sound was carried by the walls around him, multiplied in volume and frequency as they repeated into eternity. Dust filled the air and everyone's lungs, making it hard to breathe or see. The magical door opened and it brought new meaning to ancient architecture. All palaces in Garland would be like this: doors we are not aware of, rooms and treasures we haven't discovered yet. Years of Garland heritage must be still trapped beneath the overly civilized world we call home.

We walked inside and discovered a table made out of a block of granite sitting right in the middle of the room. Four pillars were set into the ground a foot away from that table, one at each corner. Every inch of the room had a thick layer of dust, which rose into the air gently when disturbed by movement or an unfiltered breath. Sunlight crept through a hole in the roof and shone on a golden-green box with engravings similar to the mysterious puzzle box I found in my foster mom's room back in Toronto. The lid opened to reveal a flat rock with words carved on it.

I took the piece of paper the priest had given me earlier and matched it to the rock. My mother had written down the inscription except for the second half, so I quickly wrote down everything and hid it inside the bottom of my shoe for safety. There was nothing else there except a small window-like passage that let air and sunlight inside the room making it naturally bright. There were broken vases on the floor and another passageway across the room that had caved in.

After an hour, we came out of the cave to further look at the inscription and properly observe every detail of the box. A group of men stood in front of us with guns stretched out toward me and the group, ready to shoot us. I stood there shocked with my arms above her head, wondering what was happening and who these people were, more importantly, how they knew where to find us.

A man dressed in a black pants, black tee shirt, whose face was hidden by a black cowboy hat, stepped forward from the crowd. A scar ran diagonally across his left eye, disappearing behind the right side of his glasses. Although there were many unsavory types with similar scars in the crowd, his gun was pointed directly at us.

The Mole

"Hello.... . You're a very hard person to find, Kailie."

"You know my name..." I asked, confused.

"Of course, I have been trying to locate you ever since you disappeared about twenty five years ago. But, I found away... an easier way... You're a splitting image of your mother. Your real mother, I mean. That's before I snapped her neck..."

"What... it was you? You're the man with the beak. I saw you in my dreams.... It was you..."

Tears came down my face, and I wept; great gulping sobs racked my chest, like a condemned man who encounters an old friend in the moments before he is hanged. I swiped at my eyes with the back of my hand, but it did little good and only smeared the tears across my cheeks like a trail of fire. Bitter regret rose up in me like acid, burning a hole through the center of me as if I were the subject of some kind of paranormal experiment. My fists clenched and unclenched at my sides as time slowed to a halt around us. Without thinking or weighing the consequences I launched towards him equipped with a ready-made stiff fist, but Adam grabbed me by my shoulders and stopped me while the guards secured their guns with their aim. Jonathan James lifted his right hand palm up, gesturing for everyone to stand down.

"Of course it was me. Just the way I killed your foster mom as well... didn't my son tell you..." said Jonathan looking at Ryan

"Your Son..."

"Ryan." said Jonathan smiling

"Ryan... What..." I screamed. My heart was breaking, and I could feel my anger in the form of fire that was coming out of my eyes, ears and every part of my body. More than the secret, I felt betrayed by the one person who I thought I might have a future with. How could he do this to me?

"You ... How could you Ryan?"

"Kailie. I had nothing to do with it. I tried to tell you that last night. That I don't want anything to do with him." Replied Ryan taking a few steps towards her

"You could have. You could have tried harder." I screamed while stepping back away from him.

"How can I tell you that my dad killed both of your mom's... I love you too much to hurt you like that... Please Kailie...I didn't want anything to do with him..."

"Enough!... Take their guns, tie them up and bring them with us... Come on men hurry up I don't have all day. Remember 6 more days." yelled Jonathan.

"No.... You can't take them...... I won't let you..." Said Ryan

"Then you shall join them." Jonathan ordered.

Before long, our hands were bound behind our backs. The blood and numbness tingling in my right shoulder made me feel like I was going to pass out. I could feel the pain in my previously dislocated right shoulder but it tends to give me trouble from time to time. The dull throbbing intensified as the restraints pulled my shoulders back and dragged me into a sitting position.

My face was pressed against the floor, and I could hear muffled sounds that seemed far away even though they came from right next to me. A blow to the head knocked me out. The others collapsed around me like soldiers who'd given up their weapons of war. But the cold, hard floor was not a fitting resting place for us.

The Family Feud

Twenty five years earlier, inside Jonathan James's home, his wife - Ryan's mother, Annie was beaten and thrown to the floor of their kitchen. She lay on the floor crying.

"Please Jon, what has gotten into you?" she said, shaking and pleading for her husband to stop.

Little Ryan comes running to save her and jumps on his dad's shoulders. Jonathan throws him on the floor with a single shove. Ryan landed head first with a thud. A streak of blood splattered across the cracked tiles, but he did not cry out or move. His mother knelt down and cradled his small body into her arms.

Annie burst into tears and clutched her child close. Her husband towering above them like an angry demon readying himself to strike again.

"You listen to me when I tell you to do something," screamed Jonathan turning towards Annie.

"You have gone mad, Jon... Just leave us be." cried Annie.

"Tell me, what the prophecy said" He yelled

"I don't know" Annie still crying

"Liar... Your father was the keeper of the legendary Manuscript. He told you with his dying breath." Johnathan said

"He just found it... You're crazy Jon... Said Annie

"You're lying, Tell me or your children are going to get it" replied Jonathan while waving a golden dagger in front of her face.

She hesitated and tried to forget what Johnathan had asked of her hours earlier but now that he waved the knife in front of her face she could not refuse him again.

"I will tell you. But, I want nothing to do with you, you will leave us alone." Annie finally said

"Yes" replied Jonathan nodding his head like he was possessed.

"The prophecy said, there is a great power that lingered in the world, and it said a woman is the guardian of that power. But, if evil stands, all is doomed. It is also said, the person who cracks the code will also have access to the greatest treasure on the planet.

Jonathan releases Annie's neck, looks straight into her eyes,

"You kept your side of the bargain. Now I will keep mine. Pack your bags and leave, take those two rascals with you.

Day 6 – Bitter Sweet

The next morning, I woke up with my hands tied to the ceiling hanging from the roof like a butcher hanging the meat out for sale, both stiff and lifeless above my head. I don't remember how I got here, nor do I remember falling to the floor unconscious. All I remember was anger, how Ryan betrayed me, and how I want nothing to do with him, yet I wanted to be with him. I found myself at a crossroads of emotions as well as in and out of consciousness. How can I possibly love a man who at some point knew about both my parents? What else did he know, and how did I not see him take advantage of me? or did I just let him because I was blinded by the love I have for him? I looked over to my left and saw my dad, the priest, and Adam in a cage, beaten. Adam was leaning against it.

"Kailie... you're awake. You okay?" asked Adam

"Yeah, I am okay. Except I have an additional person I need to kill and a headache"

"Kailie. I think he had nothing to do with this. We are alive because of him." Said Adam

"We have to go" I replied, my heart was beating faster and there was no sign I was going to reason with Adam.

"We don't know where he is," he continued.

"I don't care" I responded while examining the knots on my wrists, looking for a way to release myself.

You could see the frown on Adam's face. He turns towards his father and the priest,

"Can you please talk to her?"

I was hanging from the ceiling like a lantern, if I swing my body sideways, I would look like a bell.

"Shit, here comes the guard," said Adam

"Ohh my angle. I see you're awake" said the guard with a sly smile and lustful eyes gazing at me.

"I am no angel," I replied.

My grip tightened around the guard's neck as I swung my body forward, strangling his breath. His attempts to free himself were futile; I had locked him into place with my muscular thighs and I could feel him trembling beneath me. He desperately groped for the knife lodged in his thigh while he gasped helplessly for air. Without warning, I wrenched my body to one side with incredible force and threw the guard off-balance. A sickening thud filled the room as his limp body crumpled to the floor.

As the guards raced closer, I sprang into action. Adrenaline coursing through my veins I grabbed the rope and hefted myself up with strength I never knew exsisted, slashing through the knotted web that held me in place with one swift motion. My legs locked around the rope as an anchor and I flipped headfirst to the ground, feeling the rush of wind against my face as I plummeted to freedom.

My body tensed as I steeled myself for the five imposing guards that stood before me. Towering figures with muscled builds, they were like rock formations blocking my path. Each one of them carrying weapons and poles in menacing hands; a formidable sight to be sure. Like warriors of ages past, there was no mistaking the power and strength radiating from each figure - dauntingly double the trouble I had anticipated.

Springing across the room like a cat, I landed silently in the shadows. My karate-honed reflexes kicked in and I dispatched one guard after another with precision strikes, before making an agile leap up a ladder towards the cage. One guard managed to follow me up, but he didn't make it far as I turned back and delivered a powerful kick square to his face, sending him crashing down below. Not wasting a second, I slid down the ladder while throwing punches that knocked out the last guard.

Frantically searching for the key, my heart sank when I found none of the fallen guards had it. But then my eyes fell on an old metal object used by one of them. With trembling hands, I picked it up and pried open the lock with one powerful thrust, setting my family free.

"Good job Kailie," said Father

"How are we going to get to the location, we don't have the map. He took the box, and we have only five more days before the alignment," said Adam.

"Wait," I replied and suddenly remembered that I hid my mother's handwritten map inside the sole of my shoe.

"Look, we have the first half of the map. We know where to get the crystal," said Father

"Yes... yes... that means the map to get to the temple of light must be hidden there." Said the priest

"Temple of light?" I asked confused

"Yes the place where you have to be Kailie... during the alignment" replied the priest. While they were walking out, Father stopped and looked at Kailie.

"Your brother is right. We are alive because of Ryan"
"I don't want to think about that right now, okay."
"Where is he anyway" I asked.
"Jonathan took him, but we have to save him." Adam added.

Day 3 – The Unexpected Move

We walked for three days– each day a struggle, but we pressed on. They were the longest three days of my life, and I only hoped that when it was over we would have made it to safety. The trek through the jungle was arduous– like walking through a buffet line filled with foods you did not want to eat. We made our way up several hills before crossing a river and then continued up two more mountains– all while carrying a backpack full of supplies and with the knowledge that at any moment we could be attacked again. On the third day, night arose from the land, like ghosts escaping their coffins. We hurried up to the temple that was ruined from years of rain, sun and wind. The stones had lost their shine long ago. Jonathan James was already at the location, trying to discover the code to unlock the secret to the crystal. All four of us hid behind the bushes, going over a game plan to grab the crystal before the others.

"Okay, six men on the left, five of us here. Take out your guns and let's go!" Adam responded.

I crouched down near the bushes on the left. I was staring at a group of young soldiers playing with their rifles. On the right hid my father behind Jonathan's car and we were ready to attack. I counted down from three in my head and prepared for the fight. Jonathan James would never have expected this!

We leaped out of the darkness like shadows, our dark clothing shifting into fighting gear as we moved, but our faces not covered to hide our true identities. In less than two minutes, all twenty-five of the guards had rushed forward into firing positions. The air was thick with bullets and screams. Jonathan's guards were thrown into disarray by surprise attack. We pressed our attack before they could recover.

"Men fire, fire! We are under attack." yelled Jonathan.

A few minutes after that, everyone had been gunned down except for the few of us who were still alive. Ryan appeared from behind a tree with that look on his face that he always gets when he knows he didn't do something wrong; the kind of look where you know he has just done something right. He stood there, hands in his pockets and gun pointed at Jonathan, who darted around behind a stump, out of sight. I smelled the cordite as each missed shot ricocheted off the surrounding trees and into the forest clearing.

Jonathan was sniveling like a scared dog and pulled out his pistol from his concealed holster on his ankle. He turned toward my father and fired a single shot into his chest, dropping him cold to the ground. Blood leaked out from beneath my father's shirt and onto the dirt as he fell to the floor.

"I killed your father, and I killed your mother, now it's your turn!" he said with an evil laugh as he turned towards me with his gun aimed directly between my eyes.

As soon as I heard those words, tears rolled down my face. My father was on the floor, and Ryan and Adam were running towards him. My heart sank in such a way that a child who had lost one of their parents should never have to feel. Even though

I have felt this pain before, it was a feeling I could never get used to. Jonathan was still pointing his gun at me; he had not moved from his spot, and I was completely blindsided as I paid attention to my father. Even with three armed men pointing their guns at me, all I could think about was how badly I wanted to cry and scream for help for my father, but I was frozen.

"Don't you fucking move." Jonathan said. My eyes widened as close range he turned into plain sight right next to where my father lay dying on the ground.

"Stay back!" He ordered Ryan and Adam, as they started to take cover behind a propane tank.

Suddenly, time slowed down for me like watching something being played in slow-motion like a movie. I saw Jonathan squeeze the trigger, almost slow-motion like and the shot fired at me but no pain came yet. Tears poured from my face as I jerked coming out of my daze and quickly realized that he missed his target.

"You will pay for this." Jonathan said pointing his empty firearm at Ryan.

I ran toward Ryan and skidded to a stop. I lifted his arm and saw the long, wet red furrow that was leaking blood onto the ground—how could there be so much of it? As my hand slid down his arm to the wound I felt something warm and sticky hit my fingers. The skin of his shoulder had been stretched apart by the bullet. His skin was torn but intact, like two pieces of paper stuck together with something wet on both sides, which I feared was muscle tissue.

When Jonathan fired again I ducked into crouch position behind a nearby car before realizing that he wasn't aiming at me at all. His next shot thudded into a tree trunk about a foot from Ryan's head.

I looked at Ryan in surprise, my heart pounding against my chest. Even after everything that had happened between us, it was clear that our feelings for each other hadn't changed. Ryan's agitation only added to the tension already thick in the air. Jonathan fired his gun at me again, hoping to take me out while I was down. But as the trigger clicked, the sound echoed – there were no bullets left.

"You're as weak as your mother, Ryan!" Jonathan yelled, spittle flying from his lips.

I have had enough of this man, enough of him killing the people I loved. I wouldn't let him take Ryan away from me too. With a rage I couldn't control, I leapt towards him and tackled him to the floor with a sickening thud. My fists flew before I could think, striking flesh until Jonathan lay still and unconscious beneath me. How could I possibly kill my boyfriend's father? In that moment, I knew that despite everything, I was still more human than Jonathan would ever be.

Forgetting all that stood or fell in those last few moments of chaos, I ran towards my father and held his hand tightly.

"You will be okay, dad. We will get help."

"Kailie, I found you! Look at the beautiful woman you have become. If your mother was here, I know she would be very proud as I know I am. Please take care of yourself and remember that you are loved, always have been. You found your family, but most importantly, you found happiness. Enjoy it. This is the happiest day of my life because I know both of them are okay." said father.

He then looked at Ryan and took his hand and put it on top of mine and smiled.

"Kailie, finish what you started, make my death mean something; find the crystal before they do, your journey has just begun. Because…" and with these words he closed his eyes forever.

"dad.. dad.. because what.. " I asked softly asking him to finish his sentences while whipping the tears off my face. There was nothing but a slight wheeze rattling out from his lungs as he laid on the floor.

My heart was heavy. It was pounding with rage, disappointment and sadness all at the same time. My whole body ached from the sadness that flooded through me. I don't know how much more I can take. If there was a curse of a crystal this would be it.

"His life didn't have to end this way" I said, sobbing next to my father's lifeless body.

"It wasn't Kailie, he found you" said Adam while placing his hand on my shoulder.

I took a deep breath while Ryan helped me up. Ryan hugged me and kissed me all over my face wiping my tears away and finally hugging me letting me know that I was going to be OK.

"Are you OK to go on, Ryan with your arm"

"I'm alright. Just a scratch"

"Children, my work here is done…" said the priest

"what… but you have to come. how do we know where to go…" I replied

"Trust yourself, and all the pieces will fall into place, there is much to be done if things don't go our way. We have to prepare for the worst. Your father trained you well." The priest spoke these words and walked down the path in front of him leaving the rest of us behind.

The Last Army

After defeating Jonathan's army, we went inside the temple, thinking we would find Jonathan again as I didn't kill him, or better said I couldn't kill him, but he seemed to have disappeared. The temple was a ruin; it had been abandoned for centuries. The walls were covered with detailed carvings of lions and women holding flowers which clearly indicated the perfect craftsmanship in the early ages. The women were said to be wearing a transparent blouse and the carvings looked unclothed. The lions on the other hand seemed calm as if they were protecting something in complete watch mode. We entered through a staircase made out of the rock that led into a large room with tall pillars and a huge statue of the warrior Awana seated on a lotus flower.

"This seems to be a dead end," Kailie moaned. No doors, no passageways; nothing.

"Look," Adam said, pointing towards the lotus platform just above me. On the side of the lotus was an old stairway, not more than ten small stairs, steep and tall steps, it can barely be seen as it had been destroyed over the years.

"That means there should be a door somewhere here. The

stairs has to lead somewhere right?"

Ryan searched for clues around that area as I stared at my mother's piece of paper. The handwriting indicated a room behind a flower. From the bottom, two separations to your right, four separations up, and one separation to your left, I read out to Ryan and Adam who ran their fingers over every inch of rock searching for some sort of hidden button or lever like in an adventure story book. Finally, they caught on to something solid. They pushed against the walls until they found what felt like a switch. Suddenly, dust filled the air as it made a big roar of noise. A staircase had appeared below them.

"Well, this looks familiar," said Ryan.

We found ourselves on a path of a dark passageway, where the only way showed to us was through our trusty flashlights. The light from it created a tunnel around us as we made our way down the staircase into the large room below, which appeared to have ancient guardians in place with spears and knives. It seemed like the giant statues were guarding something. In the middle of the floor was a wide, flat rock that glowed with a soft blue hue. I stepped up toward the rock while Ryan and Adam stood behind me ready to fight if something were to happen. On the rock it had a picture of a person pushing it towards the ground and behind it was a picture of a small pond. In front of it was an item shaped like a sun that indicated brightness in the picture.

"Okay guys here goes," I said while pushing the button. The tall rock made a small part of the floor disappear and it filled with water. Through the water came another pillar and on it was a shiny object, it was indeed the crystal. I stood there looking at the beauty and the light it created. But, not for long, it felt like the roof was about to fall on our heads. I could see the rock statues of the ancient guards were starting to awaken.

"Shit!!" said Ryan, tightening his grip on his gun.

"Kailie, hurry up we gotta get out of here" yelled Adam while he prepared himself to fight. I quickly reached for the crystal along with the second map and placed it in my backpack. We all took out our guns and were ready to defend ourselves while running outside the temple.

"They are gaining on us." Yelled Adam. The three of us started to run while dogging the walls and the roof that was coming down on us. We tripped on the already fallen rocks while shooting at the awakened stone soldiers as we continued to run outside as fast as we could. Momentarily, as the three of us exited the cave and the guards stopped chasing us. It appeared the guards were only limited to the cave they were in.

"What the hell was that?" Ryan said, catching his breath. I took Mom's paper out to see where she had stopped writing and I read out the last sentence.

"Ancient warriors guard the light, Death will come upon sunlight."

"Great. You should have read that part before we decided the guards were welcome to kill us" said Adam

"Funny. I said, rolling my eyes." Alright let's start walking. This place is three days away and we have only two days left. So, I suggest we run." Ryan said

Day 2 – The Little Girl

I walked day and night through the thick of trees, my feet slapping down on the mud-covered path, for what seemed like days. Finally, I reached a small village with not more than five houses, each made of clay bricks that had been pressed by hand into the shape of buildings. Each house had a thick layer of leaves for its roof. The clean air was breathtaking. I finally realized how much I was deprived of it, so I took a deep breath in as if the air was limited, and exhaled slowly, enjoying every second of it. The population was a calming twenty or twenty-five people; children ran quietly between their parents' legs, and adults stood around talking to one another while children played in the dust or listened attentively to stories being told by elders. An old gentleman approached us and an elderly woman with a tray of food and water. They seemed to know us. At least I felt that way because everyone in the village was waving and smiling at us. I felt like an A-list celebrity for seconds, but then remembered we were still in Garland. An old gentleman looks back at me strangely as if he recognized me. He looked at me directly and said,

"Rest my child, you are going to need it."

I didn't think much of it then because I did look a bit tired. The weariness weighed like a stone, pulling the skin beneath my eyes down and making my limbs heavy. But, when we were seated outside watching the children play, one child came up to me with her cheeks red and eyes wide,

"Please save us. You're the only one who can," said the little girl.

Her voice was as small as a cricket's chirp, but it carried an intensity that made my blood run cold. I just stood there stunned, how did she know who I am? Was I the only one who didn't know? The entire village seems to know who I am, everyone except me. My heart raced with a sudden fear that threatened to overwhelm me, but outwardly I tried to maintain my composure, looking around at the other villagers scattered around area. They all looked normal enough, chatting idly about what they'd eaten for breakfast or the weather forecast for tomorrow morning– but perhaps their pleasant expressions hid something more sinister beneath them.

* * *

That night, I slept hugging my backpack, which was the closest I had been to a comfortable pillow in a long, long time. We were halfway up the hill behind the village by sunrise, although it wasn't as cold as it had been earlier, we could still see our breath in the air. The morning light filtered through the sheer curtains hanging from the windows of the hut and onto the beam sticking out of the ceiling.

I walked out of my hut with my coffee at 6:00am, to find that I was the last one to wake up. Ryan greeted me with a kiss on the cheek. His shoulder where he got shot was wrapped in bandages made of jungle vines and Grandma's homemade curatives. It hurt him to put his arm around my waist, but he did it anyway, lifting me off the ground into his arms and hugged me. I looked at him in concern, searching for answers behind his smile. He rubbed my face with his palm,

"Are you okay?" I whispered into his ear, brushing my fingers across his shoulder where he'd been shot.

Ryan sighed and grabbed my waist to pull me close to him,

"Yes. It hurts a bit, but it was a through-and-through wound, so I am okay."

He placed his palm against my face and kissed me on the forehead while wrapping his arms around me.

"That's not what I meant Ryan," I paused and took a deep breath.

"I know, let's talk about my family later, right now I just want you to be safe okay, but first," he pulled me close, his muscular body warm against the cool, evening air. My heart melted as he framed my face in his palms and lowered his lips to mine.

The little girl from before looked at me and smiled, pointing down the path that led from the village and up the hill behind it. She seemed to know just what I was searching for; it was as if she had been waiting for me all along. But before, I could respond, she waved back and ran away.

"Let's get going. We have less than 19 hours, or we are all dead." My voice called out to Ryan and Adam.

Part 1 – The Climb

We began climbing up the hill, through a forest of young trees and bushes so tall they brushed the sky. Through the mist clinging to the ground, I could make out ancient ruins scattered about like giant's toys. There were skeletons near these crumbling structures, as if they had been crushed or strangled by some powerful force just moments after death.

It was 10 at night, the darkest hour of the night. The white glow of lanterns shone way ahead into the distance. Our pace seemed agonizingly slow as we could only walk a few steps before stopping to catch our breath and gather our wits after hours of trudging through steep terrain. In this pitch black darkness I couldn't see my hand in front of my face, but I could tell that everyone around me was exhausted. With every step we took, small stones and rocks would roll down the slope beside us like marbles coming from the top of a pyramid of toy blocks. Every so often unknown insects crawled out from underneath our feet or down trees where they had been nesting. We were surrounded by nature's gallows and its stars above blinked back nervously through their branches as hundreds of fireflies fell in luminous trails from the sky like tiny comets that slipped between tree tops. All along these endless slopes we could hear chirping crickets and tapping tree frogs calling to each other just below the threshold of human hearing from far away.

I grasped my bag firmly as if it could anchor me to this world, and focused on taking one step after another until at 11.45 pm, we finally reached the top of the hill that seemed like the highest mountain.

A strange silence hung heavily over the temple of light, like a living veil, imbuing the meadow with mystery and magic; several leaves on the ancient boa tree were raised in salute to the sky warriors who stood watch over this holy place.

The entrance to the temple was covered with stone slabs that bore images of four tribal leaders from centuries ago representing the the four directions: North, South, East and West. There was no escape from the temple grounds; we had arrived on foot and there are no roads in that part of the forest.

We finally walked inside the temple which was untouched, not visited for centuries. If you looked back; our footsteps had been marked as the first visitors. As we walked inside the silent, dark hallway we reached three tall pillars around a triangle-shaped hole where I was supposed to stand.

Soaring over the triangular roof of the temple was another space, almost like in the ancient pyramid days. In front of that triangle was another tall flat rock that had a pocket to fit the crystal. I walked towards the space the crystal was supposed to be but suddenly, a man crept from behind and knocked the crystal out of my hand.

"Dad" yelled Ryan in surprise as he didn't expect him to be alive.

Adam and Ryan were held back by two overly developed guards. In a few minutes, the alignment would begin and they had to act fast, or they would all be dead. Their eyes darted left and right as Adam counted down from ten in his mind. When he reached five, their bodies tensed. In a flash of a moment, I saw five fingers blinking. It was Adam giving me a signal. five seconds to get ready and I nodded to indicate that I was. Then, he showed four fingers, three fingers, then two fingers, one finger, and finally, he flashed all five fingers again. As soon as Adam flashed five fingers, I kicked the crystal off Jonathan James' hand and onto the ground instantly. At the same time, Ryan and Adam overpowered the two guards and knocked them unconscious. I managed to take the crystal and ran toward the spot where the crystal was supposed to be placed during the alignment.

11.58 pm – I looked at Adam and Ryan who were standing there looking back at me not knowing what was going to happen.

"Arrrgggggggggggggggghhhhhhhhhhhh...." Yell Jonathan as he came charging towards me. The gunshot's echo roared throughout the room, and I stood there, shocked. I clenched my eyes tightly, unable to comprehend what had just happened. Every second felt like an eternity as I forced myself to slowly open my eyes. On the floor lay Jonathan James, his body motionless with a gaping hole in his chest still bleeding profusely. In despair, he turned around to see the most horrific sight imaginable—Ryan standing with a smoking gun in his hand, tears streaming down his face.

"Why Dad... why did you make me shoot you? You were everything to me! Why did you have to take away everyone from me?" Ryan sobbed in anguish.

The Alignment

11.59 pm – I frantically placed the crystal at the center of the rock pocket, feverishly reciting the sermon my mother spoke in my dreams. People murmured about my remarkable ability to remember such a long and complicated stories or paragraphs, but little did they know that I had been dreaming about it for years until I had it memorized deeply into my subconscious.

"Earth to Water, Wind to Fire
With the power that holds all life
And the help of all planets
This earth is yours to keep"

12:00 am – As soon as I finished the sermon a light from the three corners of the temple's roof and the top of the tunnel entrance, which was carved into the mountain wall, surrounded me making a triangle around me and on top of that another inverted triangle fell. It formed a star around me with six points. The light falling down made me feel warm inside; I was not sure what was happening but it filled me with wonder. With both triangles together it created a shining structure holding seven lights that then closed in on my body and shone back out towards the four warrior pillars outside who had been placed to hold back the tide of savages. The light radiated reflecting towards the warriors like rings in water to reach all creatures along with warmth and joy. It was a moment I would never forget.

I suddenly fell to the floor, trying to catch my breath. Everything went black for just a moment and then when I looked up to grab the crystal, it blew itself up like fireworks going off, preventing history from repeating itself. The blast sent shards of ice raining over the glittering pillar in which the crystal was housed. The room rumbled like thunder and shook around me. When the dust settled, a faint figure appeared at the front of the pillar. She smiled and then a bright light revealed another key that came out from inside the tall pillar. It had been buried in there.

"That is Princess Sophie. She is free" I said, still catching my breath.

"Was the crystal supposed to blow up" Asked Adam.

"I think that was her doing" replied Ryan looking at the transparent figure of the princess, and she faded away.

"Great, more puzzles," said Adam looking at the key.

I looked at Ryan while he reached for my arm helping me to my feet. I felt sorry for him, he has gone through so much pain just like I have.

"You saved my life. I'm sorry you had to come to this to stop your dad"

"Kailie. You're more my family than he has ever been. At least, my mom and sister are safe. I love you and I always will"

Ryan said while holding my neck with his hand. He brought his tender lips towards me, kissing me across the face until he reached my cheek. My knees were like jelly; they threatened to buckle beneath me at a moment's notice.

"Come on guys, now? You have to do that now? We still have more solving to do.' said Adam, smiling.

"If my dreams were ever correct, there should be a hidden door in this very room. Look for a lock" replied Ryan, still hugging me, refusing to let go. Thereafter, the three of us started to feel the walls of the room.

"Guys, come here" yelled Adam

"Two keyholes, one a normal key and the other... It's a star. What does that mean?" said Ryan inspecting the location.

"Well we know one is the key we just found, and the other" said Adam

"Kailie your necklace" Interrupted Ryan

I looked at him confused, Ryan took the chain off my neck and placed it on the carving, and turned it clockwise with the other key turning it anti-clockwise.

"You always had the key, Kailie. Your mom wasn't kidding when she said you're the key, she also meant it literally." Said, Ryan.

As we approached the end of the hallway, a thundering sound rumbled through the walls and made them shake. So much noise came from behind the wall that it sounded like a herd of rhinoceros had stampeded into the room. The walls shuddered as they parted to reveal another pathway. We didn't know how deep this new path would take us so we hesitated as we looked inside the room.

Adam took out his lighter and lit one of the torches along the wall and we walked through the path to a space. The light of the torch revealed more shadows in every nook as we walked through the winding, time-worn path and stepped down on each stone and touched every wall with its fire.

The three of us stood there, our mouths hanging open as if

we were fish gasping for air. The sudden realization of what we had found hit us like a burst of adrenaline; A room filled with gold, manuscripts, and wealth. The treasures that had been left behind was real just like all those legends about the past and the futures myths. It couldn't be defined in any way; it was fresh, unspoiled history and it belonged to the entire nation.

"Oh my god," I said holding Ryan's hand, the three of us stood there stunned, smiling, cheering, ultimately understanding that we had discovered one of the greatest treasures on the planet and it belonged to my family, but too much time had passed and there was only one thing to do with it. The only thing that could be done with such valuable material was to share it with the world.

The Morning

That morning, the little village that consisted of twenty-five people had grown to about a hundred overnight. People were coming out of their bunkers underground and climbing up hillsides, surging toward us in the distance as we emerged from a tunnel at the bottom of a massive hillside. They cheered, screamed names, cried out blessings and congratulations. Children held up small handmade signs with pictures or words on them. Adults unfolded larger handprinted posters haphazardly as they leapt forward to meet us. Adam, Ryan, and I met up with the old gentleman from the village.

His beard was white as snow and his face wrinkled with age, but when he saw us, his lips curved upward in a toothless smile. "Congratulations, princess," he said to me.

I didn't know why he called me a princess but I didn't feel like that. My biological family was so dear to me, but I loved each member in my adopted family as well. Even though they were not related by blood, they were as precious to me as any sibling could be.

"There's a lot of stuff up there." said Adam

"I know. What would you like to do with it?" Asked the priest

"Give it to the people. The King had a vision and we should fulfill it." I replied

"Spoken like a true princess, come have some tea. Your journey has just begun" said the priest smiling.

I didn't know what that meant. but for now I was just happy to be alive.

THE END

Awakened Mind - Power (Book 2)

The Celebration

The night was alive with the sound of laughter and music, and a thousand stars sparkled in the sky like scattered diamonds. Ryan and Adam surged through the crowd, spinning and twirling to the lively tempo of the mandolins and dulcimers. I watched with a smile, feeling the warmth of the fire in my cheeks and the soft grass beneath my feet.

The great crystal had been found. Its immense power and the light that spread was a testament to the power of Princess Sophia - my great ancestor, her spirit now freed from her five thousand-year imprisonment. The villagers had lit candles in her honor and placed flowers around the garden in tribute. It was a magical night that I will never forget; a night of freedom, good fortune, and hope for a brighter future.

A chorus of children's voices rose in the air, singing a song of joy and celebration. As their voices reached a crescendo, I felt a swell of emotion in my chest. I looked around the village and saw the joy in everyone's faces, and was reminded of how lucky I was to have experienced this moment. I closed my eyes and allowed the music to wash over me, letting it carry me away into a realm of peace and joy.

I had disrobed from my combat gear and dressed in a white lace dress that one of the villagers had graciously gifted me. A little girl with her hair in two braids and rosy cheeks, had come up to me with a smile on her face as she handed me a white wildflower and helped pin it to the side of my head. Princess Kailie was the name they called me, although I was from royal blood; I never wanted to be treated any differently. But for some unexplained reason, I felt obligated to protect these people, as if some unknown force wanted me to. Still, I could not help but wonder where did the crystal's power come from, and why did it choose me to stand in front of the pillar during alignment? I had so many questions that needed answers, but sadly everyone who may have held some answers had died before I had time to ask them. It was almost as though my subconscious knew they wouldn't answer anyway; and invisible cosmic energies were guiding me, telling me that there are some things that I am not meant to know yet.

My thoughts were interrupted by Ryan – my handsome, kind hearted boyfriend, who came over to asking me to dance. I grabbed his hand and swayed to the music. We twirled around like two shooting stars in sync with each other like we had done this a million times.

When the song ended, he pulled me in close and whispered,

"You look beautiful" before giving me a gentle kiss on the cheek. I blushed and returned his embrace, feeling a warmth in my heart that I had not felt in many years.

For one night, everything seemed perfect; no matter how fleeting this moment may be, it was enough to make me feel alive again – even if just for one brief moment – reminding me that no dream is too big nor too small for us to achieve if we so choose it.

A new age was dawning, one filled with hope and possibility. The great crystal's immense power and light had filled the air with a sense of excitement and promise. Yet no matter how many times I told myself this, I had this nagging feeling that something was going to happen.

* * *

That night I snuggled into Ryan's chest and drifted off to sleep. My dreams were muddled, as if my subconscious wanted me to have a little happiness before the events of the next day began. It was nice to be held by him. Slowly I focused on his breathing and fell asleep in his arms, allowing myself to be consumed by his love and warmth. As I drifted off to sleep images appeared in my dreams yet again.

The world around me fell silent. The stillness of the air was palpable, like time itself had come to a standstill. And then, suddenly, everything was flooded with light - an intense, burning brightness that seared through my vision and made every inch of my body ripple with heat. It was as if the sun had descended from the heavens and landed in my very own living room, illuminating everything it touched.

But then, just as quickly as it came, the light began to fade into darkness. Smoke filled the air, stinging my nostrils and making it hard to breathe. I could see nothing but a pair of piercing red eyes in the distance, glowing with an intensity that threatened to consume me whole. They drew closer and closer until they were just inches away from me.

My breath caught in my throat as I felt their gaze on me, sucking all the life out of me and leaving me cold and empty. I couldn't move or scream; fear rooted me to my spot and held me captive.

Just when I thought it was all over, a face appeared before me - my mother's face, screaming at the top of her lungs desperate and urgent,

"Wake up!"

Find out where Kailie's journey takes her next in
- The Awakened Mind -
The Power

About the Author

Born and raised in Sri Lanka, Ro moved to Toronto, Canada in 2010. An entrepreneur and a public speaker, she has devoted her time to uplifting children in underprivileged communities and advocating for women achievers. She is the Founder and CEO of the brand "Bellybees" with a long track record of product development, marketing, and corporate management.

She wrote her first book when she was 10 years old on top of a Mango Tree (never published or can be located). Her goal is to inspire the next generation of entrepreneurs and authors while living in simplicity with her husband, two children, and dog.

Social Media (Instagram l tiktok) - @rohanthiw

Also by Ro Wijewickrama

Poetry
- Moments in time
- We are them

Children's Picture Books
- Adventures of the Travelers – Episode 1
- Adventures of the Travelers – Episode 2
- Adventures of the Travelers – Episode 3
- Adventures of the Travelers – Episode 4

Workbooks
- Math – for kindergarten

Short stories
- Blunt force trauma